Master of Fortune

KATHERINE GARBERA

First published in Great Britain 2011
Large Print edition 2011
Harlequin Mills & Boon Limited,
Eton House, 18-24 Paradise Road,
Richmond, Surrey TW9 1SR

© Katherine Garbera 2010

ISBN: 978 0 263 21695 0

Harlequin Mills & Boon policy is to use papers that
are natural, renewable and recyclable products and
made from wood grown in sustainable forests. The
logging and manufacturing process conform to the legal
environmental regulations of the country of origin.

Printed and bound in Great Britain
by CPI Antony Rowe, Chippenham, Wiltshire

KATHERINE GARBERA

is a strong believer in happily-ever-after. She's written more than 35 books and has been nominated for *RT Book Reviews* career achievement awards in Series Fantasy and Series Adventure. Her books have appeared on bestseller lists for series romance and on the *USA TODAY* extended bestsellers list. Visit Katherine on the web at www.katherinegarbera.com

*This book is dedicated to
Rob, Courtney, Lucas, Josh
and Tabby for making our
summer in England so much fun
and for putting up with me saying
"just one more photo!!"*

Acknowledgements:

I'd like to thank my good friend
Kenny Howes for answering my
questions about the music industry;
Kenny has been rocking out for as
long as I've known him.
Any mistakes in this book are my own.

I'd also like to thank Krista Stroever
for all of her hard work on
editing this manuscript.

Also a quick shout out to my friends
who always have my back:
Nancy and Mary Louise—
you guys rock!

Prologue

"Why are we here?" Henry Devonshire asked. He sat in the boardroom of the Everest Group in downtown London. A nice view of the Thames was visible though the plate-glass windows.

"Malcolm has prepared a message for you."

"Why should we listen to this?" Henry faced the lawyer across the polished boardroom table.

"I think you'll find your father's—"

"Malcolm. Don't call him my father."

The Everest Group had always been Malcolm Devonshire's life. Of course, now that he'd turned seventy, it was no surprise that the old man had gotten in touch with him and his half brothers. He probably wanted to make sure that his life's work didn't end with his own death.

Geoff was the eldest of the three of them. Henry couldn't really say much about the other men. He didn't know either of his half brothers any better than he did their biological father. Geoff's very aristocratic English-looking nose betrayed his place in the current royal family.

"Mr. Devonshire is dying," Edmond Strom said. "He wants the legacy he worked so hard to create to live on in each of you."

Edmond was Malcolm's…butler, Henry thought. Or maybe man of affairs would be more apt.

"He didn't create the legacy for us," Steven said. He was the youngest.

"Well, he has an offer for the three of you now," Edmond said.

Henry had actually met his father's lawyer and personal assistant more times than he had his father. Edmond had been the one to deliver Christmas and birthday presents when he'd been younger.

"If you would all please sit down and allow me explain," Edmond said.

Henry took a seat at the end of the conference table. He had been a rugby player and a pretty good one to boot, but that had never gotten him the one thing he'd really craved—Malcolm's acknowledgment of him. He couldn't explain it any better than that. His own father had never recognized any of Henry's accomplishments. So he had stopped looking for it and gone his own way.

Which didn't explain why he was here now. Maybe it was simple curiosity about the old man.

Edmond passed three file folders across the table, one to each of them. Henry flipped his open and saw the letter his father had written to the three of them.

Geoff, Henry and Steven;

I have been diagnosed with terminal brain cancer. I've exhausted every avenue to try to prolong my life and have now come to believe I only have six months left.

None of you owe me allegiance, but I hope that the company that brought me into contact with your mothers will continue to prosper and grow under your leadership.

Each of you will control one of the divisions. You will be judged on the profit you make in your segment. Whoever shows the best acumen for running their segment will be appointed CEO and Chairman of The Everest Group.

Geoff—Everest Airlines. His time as

an RAF pilot and traveling the globe will serve him well.

Henry—Everest Records. I expect him to sign the music groups he's already helped make their way up the charts.

Steven—Everest Mega Stores. Hopefully his genius for knowing what the retail public wants will not fail him.

Edmond will monitor your progress and make reports to me. I would have come to speak with you today, but my doctors have confined me to my bed.

I have one caveat. You must all avoid scandal and focus on running your segment or the deal is off, regardless of profit. The one mistake I made in my life was letting my personal life distract me from my business. I hope the three of you can benefit from my mistakes and I trust you will accept this challenge.

Yours,

Malcolm Devonshire

Henry shook his head. The old man had just said he considered their births a mistake. Henry had no idea how Geoff and Steven would feel about that, but it ticked him off. "I'm not interested."

"Before you turn down Malcolm's offer, you should know that if any of you opt out, the money that was put in trust for your mothers and for each of you will be forfeit upon his death. The company would retain it all."

"I don't need his money," Geoff said.

Henry didn't either, but his mother might. She and her second husband had two sons they were raising. Though Gordon made a decent wage as head coach for the London Irish, they could always use a little extra, especially since they'd have to pay for university for those boys.

"May we have a moment to discuss this alone?" Steven asked.

Edmond nodded and left the room. As soon

as the door closed behind Edmond, Steven stood up.

"I think we should do it," Steven said.

"I'm not so sure," Geoff said. "He shouldn't put any stipulations on his will. If he wants to leave us something, so be it."

"But this affects our mums," Henry said, siding with Steven as he gave this more thought. Malcolm had broken off all contact with his mum once she was pregnant. That had always bothered him. He'd like to give her some-thing of Malcolm's…the thing that Malcolm had prized more than any of the actual living people who'd been in his life.

"It does affect them," Geoff said, leaning back in his chair as he thought it over. "I see your point. If you two are in then I'll do it, as well. I don't need his approval or his money."

"Me, either."

"So we're all in?" Henry asked.

"I am," Geoff said.

"I think he owes our mothers something on top of child support. And the chance to turn a bigger profit than he did? Now *that's* something I can't resist."

One

Astrid Taylor had started working for the Everest Group exactly one week ago, and her job as it had been described to her had sounded…like a glorified nanny but it paid well and that was all that mattered right now. She was to be an assistant to one of Malcolm Devonshire's sons.

Her experience as an executive assistant for legendary record producer Mo Rollins had ensured she'd get the job with Everest Records.

She was glad they hadn't asked too many questions about her dismissal from her last job.

"Hello, Ms. Taylor, I'm Henry Devonshire."

"Hello, Mr. Devonshire. I'm happy to make your acquaintance."

Henry held his hand out to her and she shook it. He had big blunt hands with neatly trimmed square nails. His square-jawed face sported a nose that looked as though it may have been broken more than once. Only fitting since he'd been a first-class rugby player until an injury sidelined him. He was still lean and athletic looking.

"I need you in my office in five minutes," he told her. "Bring everything you have on Everest Group Records. Financials, groups we have signed, groups we should drop."

"Yes, sir, Mr. Devonshire," she said.

He paused on the threshold before entering his inner office and smiled at her. "Call me Henry."

She nodded. Dang it, he had a perfect smile. The kind that left her feeling utterly gob smacked. Which was ridiculous. She'd read the reports in the tabloids and gossip magazines— he was a player. One with a different girl every night, she reminded herself.

"Please, call me Astrid," she said.

He nodded. "Have you been working here long?"

"Only a week. I was hired to work specifically with you."

"Good, then you won't be torn about who is in charge," he said.

"No, sir, you're the boss," she quipped.

"Indeed I am."

She started pulling together the reports he'd asked for. Since her career-ending affair at her last place of employment, she'd made a promise to herself to be utterly professional this time. She had always liked men and, to be honest, knew she flirted more than she should, but it was her way.

She watched him walk away. Flirting in the office was a bad idea, but he was charming. It wasn't as if Henry Devonshire was going to make a real pass at her. His social circles contained supermodels. But she'd always had a weakness for blue eyes and a charming smile. It didn't hurt matters that she'd had a little crush on Henry Devonshire when he'd been introduced as the starting flanker for the London Irish ten years ago.

So she was ready for Henry's requests. She had everything in a folder on her desktop and printed off the information for him. She also copied the file onto their shared server.

Her phone rang. Glancing down at the multiline unit, she saw that Henry was still on his extension.

"Everest Records, Henry Devonshire's office," Astrid said.

"We need to talk."

It was her old boss and former lover, Daniel Martin. Daniel was a bit like Simon Cowell, a record executive who turned everything he touched to gold. But when the gold lost its luster, Daniel moved on. Something Astrid had experienced firsthand.

"I don't think we have anything left to say." The last thing she wanted was to talk to Daniel.

"Henry Devonshire might feel differently. Meet me downstairs in that park area between City Hall and Tower Bridge in ten minutes."

"I can't. My boss needs me."

"He won't be your boss for long if you don't speak to me. I think we both know that. I'm not asking for too much of your time, just a few minutes."

"Fine," Astrid said, aware that Daniel could ruin her chances at Everest records with just a vaguely worded comment about her past job performance.

She wasn't sure exactly what Daniel wanted—their relationship had ended so badly. Maybe he wanted to make amends now that she was back in the music industry. At least she could hope.

She sent Henry an instant message telling him she'd be right back and set her phones to go to voice mail. Five minutes later she was walking through the green area on the banks of the Thames. Lots of office workers were sitting outside on the smoke breaks.

Astrid hurried past them looking for Daniel. She saw his honey-blond hair first. The weather was cloudy and wet today and a little chilly, and Daniel was wearing his favorite Ralph Lauren trench coat with the collar turned up.

Despite the fact that she was over him, she couldn't help but notice that he looked good. Women were watching him, and Astrid saw the disappointment on more than one girl's face when he turned toward her. In the past she'd relished the envious stares of other women. Now she knew that they had nothing to be envious of. With Daniel Martin the charm was only surface deep.

"Astrid."

"Hi, Daniel. I don't have a lot of time. What did you want to see me about?"

"What do you think you are doing working for Everest Records?"

"They hired me. I needed a job since I'm not independently wealthy," Astrid said.

"Don't be glib."

"I'm not trying to be. What are you really attempting to say?"

"That if you poach any of my clients…I will ruin you."

She shook her head. How could not know her at all? "I'd never do that. I'm not trying to get ahead by using someone else."

"Just be warned. If you come anywhere near my clients, I will call Henry Devonshire and tell him everything that the tabloids didn't uncover about our affair."

With that, he turned on his heel and walked away from her. She just watched him leave, wondering how in the world she was going to protect herself from Daniel.

Hurrying back to the Everest Group skyscraper, she took the elevator up to her floor, not talking to anyone along the way.

She stopped in the doorway leading to Henry's office. "May I come in?"

He was on the phone, so gestured for her to enter. She came in and placed the files he'd asked for on the corner of his desk.

"That sounds good. I'll be there tonight at nine," Henry said. "Two. There will be two of us."

He hung up the phone and looked up at her. "Have a seat, Astrid."

"Yes, sir."

"Thank you for the material you prepared. Before we dive into work, tell me a little about yourself."

"What do you want to know?" she asked. Somehow, blurting out her entire past history didn't seem prudent. And she'd learned that if she didn't ask for specifics on questions like that one she ended up revealing things she could have kept hidden.

She was hoping that working at Everest Records would be the buffer she needed between her past and her future. A job that would keep her so busy she'd stop worrying about would-haves and could-haves and learn to live again.

"For starters, why are you working at the Everest Group?" he asked, leaning back in his chair and crossing his arms over his chest. The tight black sweater he wore pulled against the bulging muscles in his biceps. Clearly the man worked out, she thought.

"They hired me," she said. After her talk with Daniel, she was afraid to say too much.

He laughed. "So it's just a wage to you?"

She shrugged. "It's a bit more. I really like music and being part of your team sounded like a lot of fun. A chance to see if we can find the next big thing…" She shrugged. "I've always thought of myself as a trendsetter, so now I have a chance to see if I am."

At one time she'd thought she might become a record producer. She understood the job and the hard work that went into it, but she'd figured out that she didn't have the attitude needed to make it there. She couldn't be passionate about the artists she promoted and then walk away from them when their sales started to tank. She liked to think she had integrity.

"That makes working for me easier, I think. I'm going to need you to be more my personal assistant than my secretary. You will be available 24/7. We won't be keeping regular office hours, because I mean to make this division of Everest Group into the most profitable. Do you have any objections?"

"None, sir. I was told that this job would be demanding," she said. She looked forward to it. She needed a demanding job to sink her teeth into. She needed the work to keep her so busy she never had time to think about her failed personal life.

He nodded and gave her that little half smile of his. "Normally we won't be in this office. I'd like to work out of my home in Bromley or my apartment here in London. We will mainly be listening to music acts at night."

"That's fine, sir." To be honest, she didn't need a lot of sleep.

"Good, now down to business. I need you to set up a file to keep information from several talent scouts. I am also sending you an e-mail with the people who work for me," he said.

She nodded and made notes as he continued to set out the terms of the job. Despite the fact that the papers made him out as a playboy, it seemed Henry had cultivated a network he could use for business.

"Is there anything else?"

"Yes. I've been pretty good at picking acts when I hear them at clubs, but I like a second opinion."

She nodded. "Why do you think that is?"

"Probably since I'm the typical person that most of these labels are targeting. I am young, social and know the scene." He nodded. "I think that has given me a good ear for trends. What about you, Astrid?"

"I love music." When she'd first moved to London she had been in the thick of the night-life. Her sister Bethann and she had shared a flat and worked menial jobs and went clubbing with friends most nights. But then Bethann had become a legal assistant and gotten engaged and her social life had changed. "Part of the reason I was hired was because I'd been a personal assistant to Daniel Martin."

"What are you into?" he asked. "What kind of music do you like?"

"Something with soul," she said.

"Sounds…"

"Retro?"

"No, interesting."

She left his office and tried to concentrate on the job ahead but she had enjoyed Henry— way too much for a boss. And he *was* her boss, something that she had to remember because she wasn't interested in starting over again with a broken heart and an empty bank account.

Henry watched Astrid leave. His new PA was cute and funny and a bit cheeky. Having her in his office and on his team was going to make this job much more enjoyable.

Despite the fact that many people believed him to be nothing more than a celebrity sportscaster and philanthropist, Henry did have a serious side. He certainly played hard, but few people knew he worked even harder.

It was a lesson he'd learned from his stepfather, Gordon Ferguson. He'd first met Gordon when he was eight years old. Two years before his mum and Gordon married. Gordon was the head coach for the London Irish now but back then he had been one of the assistants. He'd helped Henry hone his rugby skills and made him into one of the best team captains of his generation.

Henry's office was on the top floor of the Everest Group building. It was situated in a corner with a nice view of the London Eye across the Thames. He glanced around the nicely appointed office, feeling a bit uncomfortable. He knew he couldn't work in a place as boxed in and sterile as this one.

He needed to get out of here. But first he wanted to know a little more about his assistant and about the task he'd taken on.

At first, when he'd heard Malcolm's offer, he didn't care if he won the challenge or not, but now that he was here, his competitive instincts were rising to the fore. He liked to win. There was a reason he'd been named as RFU Player of the Year. He liked being the best. He hungered for it.

He skimmed the reports that Astrid had prepared, making notes and trying not to remember how long Astrid's legs had appeared under that short skirt she'd had on. And her smile… her mouth was full and tempting, and more than once when she'd been sitting there he'd wondered what her lips would taste like under his. Her mouth was wide, her lips plump, everything about her was irresistible.

Office romances weren't a good idea, but he knew himself and he was attracted to his assistant. He decided he wouldn't act on that attraction unless she showed some sign of interest in him. He needed her to win this challenge and to be honest, winning was more important than starting an affair.

"Henry?"

Astrid was standing in the doorway; her short curly hair brushed her cheeks. He really did like the slim-fitting skirt she wore—it was plaid and her black knee-high boots made her look tall. The plain black sweater clung to her breasts, and he realized he was staring when she cleared her throat.

"Yes, Astrid?"

"I need to pop down to legal to get Steph's offer details in to legal. You mind if I let my phone go unanswered?"

"No, not at all. That was quick." He was definitely going to like the perks that came with working in a large company. Being able to delegate tasks and have them done quickly—that was something he'd needed for a while.

Henry had been producing on his own in between handling his own endorsement deals for athletic shoes and soft drinks. He'd also hosted a kids' sports TV show that had run for two seasons. He liked the perks that went along with being a celebrity, but hadn't relished having to do so much of the legwork himself.

She smiled at him. "I aim to please."

"You've accomplished that," he said.

She left and he turned his chair so that he was facing the windows instead of watching the empty doorway. He'd always been a bit of a loner and that had suited him but having someone work for him…she was like his butler, he thought.

Yeah, right. He'd never ogled Hammond's legs. Yet he had to remember that Astrid did work for him. His own mother's affair with her

record producer had led to the end of her singing career and his birth. He wondered sometimes if she ever resented that, but she'd never
said.

He brushed that thought away. This was a
new century. Attitudes were different than they
had been in the '70s. But he still didn't want to
make Astrid feel uncomfortable in the office
with him.

At the same time he knew that he wasn't
going to be able to resist pulling Astrid into his
arms before too long and finding out how good
that sassy mouth of hers tasted under his.

His phone rang and he reached for it.
"Devonshire here."

"Henry? This is your mum."

He loved how she always identified herself
even though he could never mistake her for
anyone else. "Hello, Mum. What's up?"

"I need a favor," Tiffany Malone-Ferguson

said. "Do you know anyone at Channel Four?"

He knew a few people there. And he was afraid that this was going to be another attempt for his mother to regain the limelight. When pop stars and celebrities from the '70s and '80s had started turning up on game-style shows on Channel Four, his mum went mad. She'd said that she could return to the spotlight now that his half-brothers were older.

"I have talked to everyone I know over there more than once."

"Will you try again? Gordon suggested I start a show like that American show *The Bachelor*, but for rugby players. I know the lifestyle and I could definitely help arrange suitable girls. Not those tart scrummies that always pop up in the tabloids."

This idea wasn't half-bad. He made a few notes and asked her more questions about her idea. "I'll see what I can do."

"You're the best, Henry. Love you."

"Love you too, Mum," he said, disconnecting the call.

He held his mobile loosely in his hand for another minute until someone cleared their throat and he glanced up to see Astrid standing in his doorway.

"Yes?"

"I need your signature on these forms. The runner from talent scout Roger McMillan dropped this demo off with a note that they are playing tonight. And I'm going to need you to give me a little more information on Steph," she said, holding a sheaf of papers out toward him.

He gestured for her to come in.

"Also the head of legal wants a meeting with you to discuss contract procedures. I know you said we'd be working out of your Bromley office, but the management staff have enquired about setting up meetings with you. Do you want me to direct them to your home office?"

He leaned back in his chair. "No. I think we'd better establish a day in the office each week for meetings. I have six direct reports, right?"

"Yes, sir."

"Have them all scheduled for tomorrow," he said. He'd learned the hard way at rugby that if he didn't go for his goals he'd never achieve them. And teamwork was paramount to winning.

"Astrid, bring me the personnel files on all of the staff. After I've reviewed them, you can schedule the meetings. Does anyone have anything that's pressing?"

"Just legal and accounting. You need to be added to the signature authority card before you can sign this contract."

"Do you have that form?" he asked.

"It's at the bottom of your stack. I'll walk it down to accounting once you sign it."

He pulled the paper out of the stack and signed it. There were a few other housekeeping-type forms for him to sign. Astrid had prepared them with his name and flagged the places where he was supposed to sign.

"Thank you, Astrid," he said, handing them back to her. "You're a very efficient assistant. I'm sure Daniel was devastated to lose you."

She flushed and looked away, but didn't respond. "You're welcome, sir. Was there anything else before I go?"

He stared at her mouth for a minute, knowing his obsession with her lips was going to get him into big trouble. All he really wanted was to taste them.

Two

Astrid hoped that Henry never called Daniel to find out why she left her last job. Despite how close she and Daniel had become during their affair she knew he wouldn't give her a good reference. Hell, he'd said as much earlier.

At the end...there'd been all those sick days…. Daniel hadn't been very understanding. She wrapped an arm around her own waist as she struggled for a moment to keep the past where it belonged.

Astrid spent the rest of the day trying to stay focused on her job. But Henry seemed to need her in his office a lot as he got acclimated. And she found herself entranced just the tiniest bit.

He was smart and funny. Yet even innocent flirtations in the office were dangerous. Hadn't she learned that the hard way?

She walked down to the legal office and left the paperwork that Henry had signed with the proper legal secretary.

Henry's office was empty when she returned to her desk; she'd poked her head in his office to see if he needed anything. She'd listened to a few songs that Steph Cordo had sang…and that she'd heard on the morning talk radio.

She downloaded the song on iTunes and added them to her playlist. One thing she'd learned working with Daniel was to be very familiar with the artists and groups that label was pursuing. So Steph was the first of many new artists she'd be listening to. It would help give her a feel for what Henry liked, too.

Henry entered the office a few minutes later with three other men, none of whom she knew. He directed the men into his office.

"Hold my calls," Henry said.

"Certainly, sir. May I speak to you for a moment?" she asked.

"What's up?"

"These men aren't on your calendar…. Do you not want me to make your appointments?"

"Oh, of course I do. I'm just not used to having an assistant," Henry said.

She nodded. "Do you need anything for the next thirty minutes?"

"That's pretty specific," Henry said.

"Sorry about that. I'd like to go for lunch. My sister just rang and said she could meet me," Astrid clarified.

"Go on then. I'll be in this meeting for at least that long."

"Do you want me to bring you back something?"

"No. I'm meeting my...half brothers. That still sounds strange to me when I say it."

"I'd heard you all were getting together lately."

"Heard where?"

"Um...well, I read about it in *Hello!*" Astrid refused to be apologetic about it. *Hello!* and other celebrity magazines were a resource for people in their industry. Daniel used to have her keep clippings of their artists so they could track their popularity.

"Gossip rags?"

She arched one eyebrow at him. "Where else would I hear about your meeting them? We don't exactly run in the same circles."

He rubbed the back of his neck. "I know the feeling. They aren't my crowd either."

"No, celebrities and footballers are more your

speed," she said. "I guess that's how you have your finger on the pulse of what's next."

"Maybe. I think it's more a feel for what the public is hungry for."

He had a point. "I think you're a very savvy man."

"I am," he said. "Before you head to lunch, will you call Marcus Wills for me? I'm supposed to have drinks with him, but I don't think I'll have time between meeting with the other Devonshire heirs."

"Not a problem. Do you have his number handy? I haven't merged your contents file with mine yet," she said.

"I'll IM it to you."

"Great. I'll take care of it."

He nodded and walked away, and she couldn't help but admire his butt. He stopped in the doorway and glanced back over his shoulder. She blushed when he gave her a knowing smile.

"I guess you still work out even though you don't play anymore," she said.

"Didn't *Hello!* magazine have the scoop on my gym membership?" he asked.

She shook her head. "No, they didn't. I'm hoping to make a little on the side by selling them the exclusive story."

He threw his head back and laughed. And Astrid couldn't help chuckling along with him. He *was* fun and after the heartache she'd endured for the past year of her life she needed that.

"You'll do, Astrid."

She winked at him. "I know I will."

Henry went into his office, and Astrid made the call he'd asked her to before leaving to meet her sister, Bethann.

Bethann was sitting in the sun on one of the benches that lined the walkway along the Thames—the exact spot Astrid had met Daniel earlier. This part of London was newer and lined with glass-and-steel buildings, but across the river was the old Tower of London. Her sister looked up as she approached and waved.

Astrid hugged her sister as soon as she was close enough.

"How is the new job going?" Bethann asked.

"It's good. I think working for Henry is going to be just what I need. He's focused on signing new acts."

Bethann handed her a sandwich. "Be careful. The last job nearly ruined you."

She shook her head. It didn't matter that they were both grown woman; Bethann still thought of her as her baby sister who needed looking after.

"I am very aware of that. I just meant…never mind."

Bethann reached over and put her arm around Astrid's shoulders. "I love you, sweetie. I don't want to see you hurt again."

"I won't be," Astrid said. She'd made up her mind when Daniel had fired her that she wouldn't be used again. Not by any man. But that didn't mean she couldn't enjoy working for Henry.

Considering he, Geoff and Steve all had the same father, they didn't really have that much in common. If he had to guess why, he'd say it came down to their mothers: three very different women.

Malcolm had played fast and loose with all of their mothers. The paparazzi had photographed him leaving all of their residences, and Henry knew from things his mother had said that seeing Malcolm with his other lovers had slowly crushed her.

Tiffany had gone through a total confidence change in the six months leading up to his birth. No longer the brassy Irish singer who had melted men's hearts, she'd turned distrustful of compliments and started to doubt her own abilities as a singer.

The paps still dogged her even after she'd broken things off with Malcolm. But in later years she'd found happiness with Gordon—a kind of love, she told Henry when he'd asked her about it, that she'd never found with Malcolm. She'd said that her love with Malcolm had burned hot and fast but that Gordon was a slow burn. Henry hadn't understood that as a teenage boy, but as a man he was starting to.

He was very aware the paparazzi were probably having a field day seeing the three brothers together now, which was why they'd chosen to meet at The Athenaeum Club instead of a pub. He'd learned as a youngster that ignoring them and going about his life was the only way to be happy.

And happiness was one of his chief concerns. He saw Geoff sitting on a high stool at a table in the back of the establishment and nodded to acknowledge him.

Henry was stopped several times by fans from his playing days as he walked through the pub. Henry exchanged a few words with every one of them. Shook their hands and signed napkins and scraps of paper. His stepfather had always said that players should remember without the fans they'd be back on their local pitch playing for fun instead of money.

And his fans had made him very wealthy.

Geoff was on the phone, seated at the back of the club. So Henry took his time. Everyone always wanted to know whom he favored in the 6 Nations game—a tournament held between the first nations to play each other in rugby. Originally it had been England vs. Scotland, but over time had grown to include Ireland, Wales, France and Italy, as well. And it went without saying that Henry always favored the home team.

As he approached Geoff, the other man motioned he'd be another minute, so Henry detoured to the bar and ordered a beer. He wasn't too keen on this get-to-know-you meeting, but both Steven and Geoff had outvoted him, so to speak.

He brought his drink back to the table where Geoff was as the other man disconnected his call. Geoff stood and shook his hand.

"Where's Steven?"

"His secretary called and said he'd be running late today."

"I can't stay long. I've got things to take care of before I hit the clubs tonight. How'd you like your first day?"

Geoff arched one eyebrow at him. "Probably as well as you did. The airline is a well-oiled machine, and I think we should be able to show a large profit during the terms of the will."

Henry realized that Geoff expected to win. Probably by order of his birth he should inherit

the entire Everest Group but Henry wasn't
ready to back down and give up the fight. It
would take signing just one phenomenal group
for his segment to outperform Geoff's airline.
And Henry was damned determined to make
sure he found it.

"How's the record label?"

"Good. It's in good shape and I have the right
people in place."

"I always heard you were a team player,"
Geoff said.

"It's served me well all my life," Henry said.

"Good to hear it."

Henry had heard that Steven and Geoff were
both loners. Steven's mother was a twin. And,
according to the media, very close to her extended family.

His mobile beeped and he glanced down
to see that a text from Astrid had arrived. He
skimmed it and turned his attention back to his
Guinness. He and Geoff talked about sports

and Henry noticed that the other man was uncomfortable with him.

Geoff had grown up in the spotlight as part of the royal family. Henry wondered if being around a rugby man such as himself was what bothered Geoff. Though rugby was a ruffian sport, it had always been played by those of the middle and upper classes.

"Do you see your mum much?"

"Every Sunday for brunch," Henry said. His mother had done her best by him. Making sure that he grew up in comfortable surroundings with the family she'd created for them. Being left by Malcolm Devonshire hadn't put her off her dreams of family.

"That's good. My cousin Suzanne is a huge fan…."

"Does she want an autograph or a chance to meet her?" Henry said. His mum was just that, his mum, but he was very aware that to other people she was a pop star. And despite the fact that she hadn't had a hit in fifteen years, she was still very popular. And when he'd been in secondary school, all of his mates had listened to her records. Tiffany couldn't walk down the street without being recognized.

Geoff laughed. "She'd settle for an autograph."

"Send me her name and I'll get Mum to autograph a picture for her."

"Thanks. If there's ever anything I can do for you."

"I'll keep it in mind."

Steven showed up a few minutes later. "A girl is at the front desk asking for you, Henry."

"A girl?"

"Astrid something. I told them I'd let you know."

"Thanks. I guess that means I need to go."

"Do you?" Geoff asked. "Who is she?"

"My new assistant, Astrid Taylor."

Steven signaled the butler and ordered a drink. Geoff rubbed the back of his neck.

"Did she used to work for Daniel Martin?"

"Yes, I believe she did. Why?"

"I recall reading something in the business journal about it. She sued them because they didn't give her adequate exit benefits. Just be careful."

"I always am," Henry said. "I know a lot about building a winning team."

"I'll say. Do you have time for another drink before you go meet her?" Steven said as his drink arrived.

Henry wasn't sure and being indecisive didn't sit well with him. He shook his head. "I better not. We have a couple of meetings tonight. I appreciate the information Geoff. I'll keep my eyes open."

Geoff laughed. "I sound like my sisters passing gossip."

"You have sisters?" Steven asked.

Henry had to laugh at that. They'd been linked…well their *names* had since their birth, but they were virtual strangers.

"I have two younger brothers," Henry said.

"I'm an only child." Steven took a sip of his drink. "But we can talk about siblings later."

"I'm not sure I trust Malcolm not to throw something else at one of us," Geoff said.

"I agree. I'm surprised even being faced with his mortality has made him contact us," Henry said.

"Too right," Geoff added.

"I don't give a damn about his legacy," Steven said. "I'm in this for the money and the challenge."

Henry laughed at the way Steven said that. This man was someone who just said what he wanted, to hell with the consequences.

"I see your point."

"Good…on that note, I think you should

know that I've been contacted by a magazine… Fashion Quarterly—"

"Isn't that a woman's magazine?" Henry asked. His mum loved the magazine and read it cover to cover each month.

"Yes, it is. The editor-in-chief needed a favor from me and I helped her out in exchange for a promise to run some articles on us in her magazine."

"On us?" Geoff asked. "Everything I do has to go through the Royal Press Office."

"It's on our mums actually since it's a woman's mag but they will mention our business units and do a bit of a showcase on each one as well," Steven said.

"My mum will love that," Henry said.

"I'm not so sure about this," Geoff said.

"Just talk to her," Steven said. "We need the publicity and this is a nice angle."

"I'm in. You don't need to convince me,"

Henry said, glancing at his watch. "Is there anything else we need to discuss?"

"I like your idea of using the airlines to promote the album covers," Geoff said. "So I'll be calling you tomorrow or the next day to get a team together to move that idea forward."

"I'll look forward to your call," Henry said. "Steven, I've got a few ideas for using the Everest Mega Store to promote my newer artists. Do you have time to meet with me this week?"

"I do. Shoot me over an e-mail with your availability and we will make it work," Steven said. "I have to go to New York to check out our North American operation.

"Indeed," Henry said. "So we're doing this again next week?"

"Yes. I think a weekly check-in is a good idea," Steven said.

Henry left his half brothers and walked slowly through the club. He didn't worry about

Malcolm because that man was a stranger to him just like Steven and Geoff, and he was the type of man who didn't worry about the future. He'd take care of what he needed to.

And right now that involved finding out a little more about Astrid and her past employer.

He spotted her standing at the coat check. She was talking on her mobile and turned around as he came down the stairs. She waved at him and smiled.

He smiled back, thinking that talking to his assistant was going to be very enjoyable.

Astrid hung up the phone as Henry joined her. He looked good in his trendy casual clothing. He wore gray trousers and a button-down shirt left open at the collar with a navy blue sport coat that made his eyes seem brighter. He smiled at her as he approached, and she just stood there for a minute not saying anything.

It didn't help that he was one of the rugby

players she'd had an insane crush on when she was a teenager, which made it harder for her to see him as her boss now that they weren't in the office.

"Hello, Astrid. What did you need me for?"

"A signature. Without one your staff isn't going to get paid," she said. They all got paid monthly, so missing a pay period could put a lot of the staff in a bind. And since she'd only just started at Everest Records she didn't have the relationships needed to finesse the payroll clerks into giving her an extra day.

She handed him the papers and he signed them with a flourish. His signature had style just like the man.

Oh, for God's sake, she thought. She was developing a crush on him. On her boss! This had to stop.

"Thanks."

"No problem. Are you going back to the office now?"

"No I have a runner waiting for this packet. I'm supposed to meet you in fifteen minutes and I'd never make it on time."

"No, you wouldn't. Did you eat yet?" he asked.

She shook her head. There hadn't been time. She handed the packet to the runner she'd brought with her, and he took it and left.

"Want to grab a bite?" Henry asked. "I'm hungry."

"Sounds good."

He led the way out of the club. "Do you have a car?"

"No. I take the underground mostly. Congestion charges and parking are outrageous," she said.

"That they are. There's a congestion charge around my neighborhood. I have to pay to drive home." Traffic was a major problem in some London areas, so a charge had been introduced to ease traffic flow during certain hours.

"Not many days," she said. "I hear you get home in the wee hours of the morning."

He chuckled. "That's true. But if I kept re-spectable hours I'd have to pay."

"You do now with the job," she said.

"That's true," he said. "What about you?"

"What do you mean?" she asked.

"Is this job keeping you respectable?"

She had no idea what Henry was after with his questions. The valet brought his car around and after she was seated in the Ferrari Enzo, Henry put the car in gear. He drove with con-fidence and skill, negotiating the traffic with ease. She couldn't help but admire the way that he drove. She was beginning to believe there was little that Henry didn't do well.

"Of course it is."

"Did your last job, working for Mo Rollins's group, do the same?"

She had a sinking feeling that he'd checked her employment record. Had he found out about her affair? Bethann had suggested to her before she'd taken this job at Everest Records that she should work in another industry, but the record industry was all she knew.

"I took that job really seriously, Henry. I was a good employee and supported Daniel in every way I could."

"But he still let you go," Henry said.

"I had a health issue," she said. This was a nightmare, she thought. When she'd been in the throes of her affair with Daniel it had never occurred to her that someday she'd be answering questions about why she no longer worked for him.

Henry braked to a stop as they neared Kensington High Street. She knew he planned to check out Roof Gardens, the eclectic nightclub owned by Richard Branson, tonight.

"Babylon okay for dinner?" he asked.

"Yes." She'd never eaten at the trendy high-priced restaurant before. When she'd been with

Daniel, even when they'd been dating, they had tended to stay more to economical places. Daniel only spent money on his clients.

Henry pulled up to the valet stand and got out. Astrid climbed out on her side and wished for a moment she'd taken time to dress a bit differently for her day. She was already realizing that Henry was different. That didn't mean he would treat her better than Daniel had. This was a job, she thought. *Nothing more.* The measure of the man she worked for was better than her previous boss. And she knew she was going to have to change and probably grow a bit to keep up with him. She shifted the strap of her large shoulder bag and hurried around to the sidewalk so she was next to him.

There were a few paps—paparazzi—who took some photos of Henry. She stepped back so he could be photographed alone. He posed and talked to the photographers and signed a few autographs before reaching for her hand and drawing her up the path to the entrance.

She knew that Henry hadn't finished questioning her about her past and Daniel. She also decided if she played her cards right, she could keep him off the topic tonight.

"Does that happen to you often?" she asked when they checked their coats downstairs.

He smiled ruefully. "Yes. I'm used to it, though. My mum says that it's part of our life being in the spotlight. I grew up around it. I don't court them, but if they want a photo I give them one."

"Isn't it intrusive?" she asked.

He stopped and pulled her toward a quiet corner. "It's my life. I don't think about it. When I was a player, I didn't like them because they were a distraction and some of the other players would let the paps keep them from concentrating on the game. But now, they are what keeps my lifestyle going forward," he said.

"You're a very smart man," she said, coming to the conclusion that the showman, the charming playboy that he projected to the world was just one of the many facets of the whole man.

"Indeed. So that's why I'm not going to let you distract me from the fact that you still haven't told me everything about your last employer."

Three

Astrid tossed her head to the side and gave him a look that told him he was going to have to be subtler if he wanted to find out about her past. He nodded and took her arm leading her to the maître d' stand. They were seated shortly at an intimate table for two that had a nice view. He realized he didn't want to look at anyone but Astrid.

She was a mass of contradictions and she fascinated him.

"I think the London music scene is really hot right now. So many little local acts are making it big, not just here but in the States."

"But are they ready for it?" Henry asked.

"I'm not sure they are. You've grown up in the spotlight and you know how different it is from the paps in the States. I think that some of the groups aren't really ready to handle the fame that they achieve so quickly. And the American market can be fickle."

"Yes, they can. I've been trying to caution Steph that making it big there will mean a meteoric rise, but it could be followed by quite a crash."

"It's good that you've taken the time to talk to her. I can help with that, as well. I listened to her music earlier today and the demo that Roger dropped off. I also think I know some venues that will suit the style of music you're looking for."

"And what kind is that?"

"Something with a hook, of course, that is catchy and that people will remember. But I think you're also looking for music that has some heart to it."

He nodded. She did indeed know what he was looking for. That made him uncomfortable. He liked to play at being an easygoing guy that everyone knew and who in turn knew everyone, but in reality he kept himself distant. The only woman he could really claim to know well was his mother. And she was, by anyone's definition, eccentric.

But Astrid was different. She was calm and quiet at times. Like now.

"How long did you work for the Mo Rollins Group and Daniel Martin?" he asked. Mo Rollins was a legendary producer who had established his own label after leaving Sony-BMG. Daniel was one of his up and coming protégé.

"Only eighteen months, but I had worked as

one of the assistants to Mo's executive assistant for more than three years before that."

"Did you like it?" he asked. It made no sense that she'd leave that job and then come work for him. If she wanted to work in the music industry, then the job had been ideally suited for her. Henry told himself that he wasn't asking her because he was curious about the woman. He needed to know about her past because she was part of his team and he needed to know every nuance of his team if they were going to be a success.

"I loved it," she said, putting down her wineglass. She leaned across the table and put her hand over his. She had neatly painted nails and her hand was very soft against the back of his. Being a rugby player he'd always had calloused or bruised hands, but hers were soft and cool.

"I know you want to understand why I left such a high-profile job. There's a lot to it.... It was a highly personal health issue and I just don't—" She broke off, tears filling her eyes.

Henry turned his hand over under hers and held hers loosely in his grip. He understood about secrets and personal issues. He could hold off for now, but before too long he would know *all* of Astrid Taylor's secrets. HR had screened her and wouldn't have hired her f there was anything untoward in her past.

"Very well. Tonight you are going to meet Steph Cordo. Part of your role will be to act as an assistant to my stable of artists until they hire their own people," Henry said.

"Right. I've done that type of work before. I can handle that."

"I know you can handle it, Astrid. You're very adept at doing what needs to be done," he said.

She flushed. "My sister says it's a gift."

"Really? Why?"

"Um…I was always a bit of a suck up when

we were younger. But being nice does open doors," she said with a wry little grin.

"Indeed."

Henry noticed he was still holding her hand. He stroked his thumb over her knuckles and watched her face. She flushed again and then pulled her hand back. She licked her lips, which were wide and full. Her mouth moved and he knew she was saying something, but for the life of him he couldn't concentrate on her words.

All he could do was watch them move. Stare at her white teeth and very pink lips and wonder how her mouth would feel under his.

"Henry?"

"Hmm?"

"The waiter asked if we wanted dessert," she said.

"Sorry, mate. I'm good. Would you like something, Astrid?"

She shook her head.

He asked for the check and Astrid excused herself to go to the ladies' room. It was odd that the old man had decided to get in touch with him now, but Henry thought that the job at Everest was going to be a fun challenge.

He'd long since stopped thinking of Malcolm as any type of relation. The man had sent gifts at birthdays and Christmases over the years, but Henry didn't really know him. He'd always been a sort of Dr. Who character that came in and out of his life with no real notice.

But Henry felt the need to know more about him now. Malcolm held the key to any future success his team would have because of the will. His BlackBerry rang and he glanced at the screen. Henry had a firm policy of not talking on his cell phone when he was out with another person.

Alonzo, one of the men he paid for tips on new bands, sent a text message that he had a group that Henry should check out playing later in the evening at a club a few blocks from where they were. Henry noted it.

He wasn't one for letting any leads slip by him. Maybe that was why he hadn't had a problem transitioning from rugby player to entrepreneur back when he'd first retired.

He glanced up as Astrid was walking toward him and simply watched her. She moved like many women did when they knew a man was watching. Her hips swayed languidly with each step and her arms moved by her sides.

"You're staring at me, boss man."

"You're a very pretty girl, Astrid."

She tipped her head to the side. "Thanks, I think."

"You think?"

"Is it a genuine compliment, or are you just buttering me up for some nasty assignment?" she asked.

He shook his head as he stood. He put his hand on the small of her back and directed her out of the restaurant. He knew she didn't need his hand on her to figure out which way to go, but he wanted to touch her. There was something…almost irresistible about her.

"It was genuine. If I ask you to do a task you find distasteful it won't be hidden in between something pleasant."

She paused and glanced back at him. He stopped, and their faces were very close together. "Promise?"

"I promise," he said. Before he could say anything else, a flashbulb blinded him. He turned to face the cameraman, but the person was retreating.

They met Roger McMillan, a friend of Henry's, at the first club they entered. The place was crowded, as was to be expected, but they were immediately ushered to a VIP area cordoned off by velvet ropes.

Roger shook her hand and said something to

her, but she couldn't hear him over the music. She nodded and would have excused herself but Henry grabbed her hand and led them to a table in the back.

It was a little quieter and Roger introduced himself again.

"Astrid Taylor," she said.

"She's my assistant. You will be calling her every morning by ten with any new groups you've identified."

"Got it. There's not much going on here tonight. But the deejay has a tip for us on a hot new group. Once he takes a break, he's going to come and meet us."

"Sounds good," Henry said.

"I'm going to make the rounds, see if there are any artists here tonight that you should meet," Roger said.

He excused himself and left the table. Astrid realized that Henry wasn't going to ease into his new job but had already hit the ground running. Unlike Daniel, he knew how to delegate. Henry wasn't all about himself.

"Why are you watching me like that?" he asked.

"You aren't going to follow Roger or send me after him?"

"Why should I? He knows what's expected of him and he's never let me down."

She shook her head. "That kind of attitude is different."

Henry nodded. "Everything I need to know about life I learned on a rugby pitch."

"Truly?"

"Indeed. The first thing I learned is that if you don't trust your teammates then you don't trust yourself. You can't be everywhere. So you must surround yourself with like-minded people."

"So many people in this business are...elbows out. You know, always trying to shove themselves to the front of the line. When I worked for Daniel and Mo Rollins there was always a list of calls to be made just to make sure that people were doing what they were supposed to do."

Henry leaned in closer. "Is that one of the reasons why you left?"

"No. It isn't," Astrid said.

Henry put his arm around her shoulder and drew her back against the banquette. "I can't be successful until I know every member of my team—their strengths and their weaknesses."

"I don't have any weaknesses from my past that you need to worry about, Henry. I'm telling you everything you need to know about me."

Henry stroked one finger down the side of her face and she shivered. She wanted to rebuild her life and she couldn't do that if she was lusting after him.

"Let me be the judge of that," he said.

It took just those few words to convince her

that he wasn't the easygoing guy he wanted the world to think he was. Henry Devonshire was a man used to getting his way. And right now that meant he was going to try to uncover her secrets.

Her secrets.

She had so many. And she knew there was no way in hell that she was going to trust Henry Devonshire with them. Men had let her down. Not her dad. No, her pop was a stand-up sort of guy. But the men—man—she'd met since she'd left home… Daniel Martin had broken her ability to trust. He had shown her that not all men rewarded her trust in them.

"Not just yet," she said.

He nodded and sank back into his own chair. "You don't trust me."

"I don't know you," she said. That was one lesson she had learned. Not everyone she met had the same feelings of loyalty toward their friends that she did. And until she really had

Henry's measure as a man, she wasn't about to trust him.

When she'd first started her affair with Daniel, she'd known it was risky to be involved with her boss, but the thrill of falling in love with someone as dynamic as Daniel had offset that. More than that, she'd also had her belief that Daniel was falling for her. And that made the risk more manageable—only after she found herself dumped by Daniel and pregnant with his child did she realize that her sense of loyalty was different than his.

"Point conceded," Henry said. "What do you think of this deejay?"

"He's okay," she said. "His sound is very funky and modern, but there's nothing to make him stand out from any of the other clubs."

"I agree. He's just one of the crowd, but he does have a good ear. We're looking for artists who can stand out in the crowd whether they are loved or hated, as long as they are noticed.

I'm going to chat with him and see if he has any tips for me."

It was twenty minutes later when they left for a club in Notting Hill. Cherry Jam had a New York City feel to it. She saw two mates from her old clubbing days, and Henry nodded her off as he was dragged into a rugby conversation with Stan Stubbing, a sports reporter for the *Guardian*.

Molly and Maggie Jones were sisters who were only eleven months apart. Maggie, the older of the two, was actually Astrid's age.

"Astrid! What are you doing here?"

"Working! I'm here to check out the bands."

"I thought you'd stopped working for that record producer," Molly said.

Astrid swallowed. She had become used to the questions about her leaving Mo's organization, but she'd never really figured out a good answer. "I just started a new job with Everest Records."

"Which explains why you are here with Henry Devonshire. He is one cute guy."

"He's my boss," Astrid said.

"He can still be cute," Maggie pointed out.

"True. What are you drinking?" she asked her friends.

"Pomegranate martini. Want one?"

"I'd love one," Astrid said.

Molly went to the bar to get her one, and she and Maggie looked for a place to sit but the club was packed and the long, low tables were all full.

She glanced at the VIP area, where Henry had a table with Roger and a woman who looked familiar. He waved her over as soon he glanced up.

"Go on," Maggie said.

"You can come with me. Henry won't mind."

"All right then. Here's Molly with your drink," Maggie said.

Henry was seated at the head of the U-shaped

booth and Roger sat on one side. Astrid slid in next to the woman, Molly followed her and Maggie sat next to Roger.

"Astrid, this is Steph Cordo. Steph, this is my assistant Astrid."

Astrid shook the other woman's hand. She was older than Astrid expected her to be. Most pop singers seemed to be sixteen these days, but Steph was at least twenty-five. Her eyes said she'd experienced a lot of life.

"Nice to meet you."

"You, as well," Steph said.

"These are my friends Maggie and Molly Jones," she said to the table.

Once everyone was introduced, Roger and Henry went back to discussing the music business and Astrid turned to Steph.

"Tomorrow we're going to have a lot for you to do. Did Henry mention that to you?"

"Yes. He also said you'd be setting up an appearance at the Everest Mega Store."

"I will? I mean, of course I will. We can talk about that tomorrow. When is the best time to reach you?"

"Anytime except the afternoon. That's when I sleep."

Maggie laughed. "I wish I had that schedule."

Steph flushed a little. "I've always been a night owl, and my mum's a nurse. She used to work the overnight shift when I was growing up…. I guess I developed the habit early of staying up to talk to her."

"My dad worked nights for a while before he bought his own cabs. We used to have breakfast every morning before school," Astrid said.

Her dad had been a cab driver while she was growing up. He still owned a cab but had hired another man to drive it when his health had started to fail. Her mum had been a stay-at-home mum while she and Bethann were in primary school, then she'd gone back to teaching.

"Me, too. My mates were always having dinner with their folks, but for us it was breakfast."

"Us, too. When my dad got sick, that was the one tradition we kept to even when he was in hospital—Bethann and I would make sure we stopped by at breakfast time."

"What was your dad in hospital for?"

"Diabetes," Astrid said. "He's had it for most of his life, but he hates to eat right."

"My mum would have given him hell if he'd been one of her clients. She is adamant that you can't neglect your health, and I've picked up a few of her healthy habits," Steph said.

"Me, too. I think because my dad's health has always been so bad I'm really aware of what I'm eating and the effect it has on my body. I don't want to end up like him if I can help it."

"Is he bad?" Steph asked.

"Wheelchair bound," Astrid said.

"How has your family handled that?"

"My sister and I take turns going down and helping our mum out. And we paid to have parts of the house converted so he could use his wheelchair in it. The hallways were so small."

"I know what you mean. My mum is always saying this country is behind the times with awareness for the disabled."

"The thing is, if my dad had been better about eating right he might not have needed the wheelchair. I didn't mean to say that he could have helped it—"

"I know what you mean," Steph said. "You just want to prevent that from happening to you if at all possible."

"Exactly. I just want to live a normal life."

"I've always been baffled by the words *normal schedule*. No one really has one.

But I think we find 'normal' for ourselves," Steph said.

"Is Astrid keeping you entertained?" Henry asked.

"Very much. I like her. She's not like the other people who I've talked to in this industry."

"In what way?" Henry asked.

"She's real people." Steph said.

Astrid smiled and realized that she could be friends with this woman. Something she'd sort of picked up from Steph's chart-topping song "My World."

"It's going to be nice working with you," Astrid said.

"I think so, too," Steph said.

The conversation drifted in another direction and Steph turned to talk to Henry. Astrid chatted a bit with Maggie before the other woman and her sister had to leave. She watched them go, regretting that she'd shut herself off from her old life when she'd lost her last job.

Being pregnant and having the complications she'd had had put an end to her nightlife. And then the scandal and rumors about her firing and her relationship with Daniel had made her want to hide.

And she had, by retreating to her home and not talking to friends.

The need to run and hide from everyone meant that she'd been missing out on a part of herself. She vowed never to do that again.

"Sorry, Astrid, but could you let me out?" Steph asked.

"Certainly." Astrid scooted out of the booth until Steph left and then sat back down.

"Pretty good evening so far. I think you have convinced Steph to sign with Everest Records. She was afraid that we'd be all corporate and not 'get' her music."

"Of course we won't be. I like her. I wasn't trying to convince her of anything."

"I know, that's why it worked. I think you are going to be an asset to my team," Henry said.

Astrid smiled and felt a flush that came with knowing she'd done a good job. That was it, she told herself. It had nothing to do with the fact that Henry had leaned in close to her and had his arm around her shoulder.

"I want to hit one more club before calling it a night," Henry said. "You up for that?"

She thought about her after-Daniel routine— evening television programs followed by a cup of chamomile tea and bed by eleven. For the first time since she'd lost her baby she felt alive. Really alive.

"Yes, I am."

"Good. Let's go," Henry said.

They talked a little more about what he wanted on their way to the next club, and Astrid was careful to listen to what he said. Throughout the rest of the evening he didn't push anymore to find out why she'd left Mo Rollins's organization, and she was glad of it.

She knew, though, that it was a temporary reprieve. Henry was going to get the answers to his questions. He was simply biding his time and letting her get to the point where she was finally comfortable.

She thought she'd have weeks to get to the point where she'd casually mention Daniel and the fact that over the eighteen months she worked for him their relationship had progressed from professional to personal, but that all changed when they left their third club of the evening and she stepped out into the night air and nearly collided with a tall, broad-shouldered man.

"Sorry," she said, glancing up into eyes that were very familiar.

"Astrid? What are you doing here?" Daniel asked.

"Working," she said.

"For me," Henry said, stepping behind her and putting his arm on her elbow as he drew her away from Daniel.

Four

Henry didn't like the way the other man was looking at Astrid. It was more than the way an ex-boss should. Over the course of the day he'd started thinking of her as his. Not in a sexual way…well, not completely in a sexual way. And he could tell from the frozen expression on her face that this man wasn't a friend of hers.

"Henry Devonshire," Henry said, offering his hand to the man.

"Daniel Martin."

Suddenly a lot of things fell into place. Astrid's old boss was more than her boss. No wonder she'd been reluctant to talk about him.

"I've heard a lot about you."

"You, as well. Steph Cordo was quite a coup for you. A lot of producers are envious they didn't get the drop on you."

Henry smiled affably. His time in the spotlight taught him how to conceal what he really felt about others. And he didn't like the brash American Daniel. He rubbed Henry the wrong way.

"Henry's got an eye for talent."

"Let's hope he can also spot the slackers," Daniel said.

Astrid flinched and drew her handbag closer to her body. "I've always known how to build winning teams. There's our car. Good evening, Daniel."

Daniel nodded, and Henry led Astrid to the valet stand where his car waited. She was eerily silent for someone he'd come to expect to be sassy and spunky. Was the cheeky girl he'd come to know just a façade, and was this introspective woman the real Astrid?

"Daniel was the reason you left your last job," Henry said.

"It was attendance, like my record stated. I know that Daniel wouldn't have given me a recommendation."

"He didn't."

"Figures."

"How long were the two of you involved?" Henry asked.

"Why do you think we were?"

Henry gave her a shrewd look. "Ex-lovers make everyone react differently than ex-bosses. So...how long were you two involved?"

"Too long," Astrid said. "I...I'm not normally

like that. I really thought that Daniel was a different man."

Henry sensed that about Astrid. She was funny and outgoing, but he had noticed earlier in the evening that she kept a barrier between herself and others. He'd recognized that trait mainly because he always did the same.

"Do you want to talk about it?" Henry asked.

She shook her head and clenched her hands tightly on her lap. He knew that she was trying to control her reaction to seeing her ex-lover.

Henry said nothing, just kept driving. He didn't know where Astrid lived, and he didn't want to interrupt her in the middle of whatever she was going to say.

"I always thought… Well, that hardly matters. Where are we going now?" she asked.

"Home. But I'll need your address."

"You can drop me at the nearest Underground."

"No, I can't. They've stopped running at this hour."

She glanced at her watch and then shook her head again. "You're right. I live in Woking."

He put her address into his Sat Nav system and then followed the directions of Mr. T's voice. As he expected, Astrid laughed a little the first time the recorded voice told him to "turn around, fool."

"I can't believe you have that rude voice on your Sat Nav."

"It's Mr. T. That's his persona—big tough guy."

"I don't get it. But then Americans are very different, aren't they?"

"Some. They don't get rugby, which makes no sense at all to me."

She smiled again, and he felt good for having made her smile. "I guess they are just daft."

"Must be. Do you follow rugby?" he asked.

"Some," she said, blushing the slightest bit.

He could only see the rise in color as he braked to a stop for the traffic light. "I used to when I was younger."

"Which teams?"

"England, of course, in the 6 Nations."

"Have you been to any games?" he asked.

"A few. I used to be really into going to the games at Madejski Stadium to watch the London Irish play."

"Why'd you stop?" he asked. His old team was still a contender.

"My dad got too sick to go. And it was always something I did with him."

"Your family must be very close," he said.

"Why do you say that?" she asked.

"You had lunch with your sister, went to games with your dad."

She shrugged. Something he noticed she did a lot when she was evading answering a question. "I suppose we are. What about you?

Your mum is Tiffany Malone. That had to be exciting."

"She's still my mum," he said. "We're quite close, actually. She loves being a mum and smothers my brothers and I with her mothering."

Astrid smiled again. "Are you a bit of a mummy's lad?"

"What do you think?"

She tipped her head to the side as she studied him and, having lightened her mood, he felt as if he was seeing the return of Astrid. Not that tight-lipped stranger whom Daniel Martin had evoked.

"I think you are a man who knows very much what he wants and probably doesn't look to anyone for approval."

He nodded. "Damn straight. Now which place is yours?"

She pointed to a modern block of flats and he pulled into the parking lot. She reached for her door as he turned off the car. He got out and met her as she exited the car. It had started to drizzle on the drive, and the rain made her hair curl.

She stared up at him for a minute, chewing on her lower lip. "Thank you for the ride home. And for...well for being so nice about every- thing. You made seeing Daniel again bearable for me."

"You're welcome," he said. He cupped her elbow and led her to the entrance of the building.

"Well, good night, then," she said.

"Good night, Astrid," he said. But instead of doing the smart thing and letting her enter her building, he touched the side of her face and lowered his head to kiss her.

Astrid leaned up into Henry's kiss. He didn't put his arm around her, but kept one hand on her face. His lips rubbed lightly over hers, and she stood on tiptoe to get closer to him. His lips were soft and provoked a slow burn.

The reaction of his mouth on hers sent tingles down her body and she opened her mouth on a sigh. She tasted the minty crispness of his breath before his tongue brushed over hers. Forgetting everything, she felt only his mouth on hers.

The hand on her face slid to the nape of her neck, and he held her firmly as he took complete control of their kiss.

She couldn't think.

She didn't want to. She'd watched Henry all day and night wondering what it would be like to be in his embrace, and now she knew. It was intense.

He smelled earthy and masculine. His cologne was expensive and crisp—she suspected it was custom-blended just for him. She closed her eyes to focus her senses in the experience.

He pulled back, and she opened her eyes to see him staring down at her. He said nothing but rubbed his thumb over her bottom lip and then stepped away from her.

"Good night, then," he said.

She watched him walk back to his car and realized she was still standing there like a ninny. She unlocked the lobby door to her flat building and walked in without looking back at him.

Danger loomed—real danger of falling for Henry Devonshire. A man who would never see her any differently than Daniel had. How could he? His mother was a pop star, his father was a billionaire entrepreneur and she was the daughter of a schoolteacher and a taxi driver.

When was she going to learn?

Why did she have a weakness for men who were…

"Not good for me," she said out loud.

She kicked off her shoes as she entered and

dropped her keys on the kitchen counter. It took her fifteen minutes to get ready for bed, but once she was there she couldn't sleep. She just kept reliving, not the encounter with Daniel, which she'd expected, but the kiss with Henry.

She'd never been kissed like that before. It had been too intense. Her vows to herself about not getting involved with men she worked with melted away.

She drifted off to sleep and woke early for work. She dressed in an ultraprofessional suit that she'd worn to her interview with Malcolm Devonshire's assistant Edmond. That suit was her armor when she needed to be professional. Bethann called, but Astrid let it go to voice mail because Bethann could always tell when something was going on in Astrid's life. Her older sister had known her affair with Daniel had gone wrong just from the way Astrid had said hello.

The train was busy, but that was normal for the morning. She knew she was going to have to figure out an alternate way to handle her commute once she started going out at night with Henry. She tried to fill her mind with to-do lists and other meaningless tasks, but the one thought that kept circling around was what would happen when she saw Henry.

How was he going to treat her today?

Her mobile rang again and she hit the quiet button. The part of the train she was on was a quiet zone, so she couldn't talk to Bethann even if she wanted to. A minute later she received an instant message on her Smartphone. They each had a BlackBerry so could use the Messenger on that.

Bethann: Stop ignoring my calls.

Astrid: I'm on the train, Bethann. I can't talk just now.

* * *

Bethann: Where were you last night?
Astrid: Working.

Bethann: I left you a voice mail at home...I'm worried about you. I think you should have taken a job in my office.

Astrid hadn't even seriously considered working with her sister at the law office where Bethann was a solicitor. She loved Bethann, but the other woman was demanding and very bossy. If they worked together, Astrid was afraid she'd lose it and say something that would hurt her sister's feelings.

Astrid: I like working in the music industry. My stop's next. Daniel contacted me and threatened to tell Henry awful things about me.

* * *

Bethann: I'm going to contact his office today. We filed a wrongful termination.

Astrid: I know but the fact that I settled makes it seem like there was something untoward between us.

Bethann: There was.

Astrid: Stop being a cow about that. I need you to just tell me everything's going to be okay and the one mistake I made falling for that man isn't going to ruin the rest of my life.

Bethann: Love, don't say things like that. You are on a better track now. Sorry for being bossy.

* * *

Astrid: No problem. Sorry for getting all emotional.

Bethann: Have a good day, sis.

Astrid: You too. TTYL.

She entered her office to find three e-mails from Henry, the last one saying he'd be in the office later this morning.

She stashed her handbag and started to work. Tried to get into the flow of the office. There were a couple of coworkers that she'd started being friendly with in the kitchen area where the coffeepot was kept, but this morning she kept to herself. Stayed at her desk and just worked.

She had made mistakes with Daniel. At first their relationship had been like this one with Henry, and now she was afraid of repeating those same mistakes. She refused to let that happen.

Just because they spent every eight hours together in the office and then most evenings together didn't mean they were growing closer. She had to remember he'd been happy last night because she'd helped convince Steph to sign with Everest Records.

Daniel had been happy with her too, and then she'd started to fall for him. Or rather let him seduce her. She couldn't make that mistake again. Henry was her boss and unless she wanted to go back to Farnham with her tail tucked between her legs she needed to make this job work.

She wasn't going to have that fairy tale happily-ever-after with Henry even if he was different from Daniel. She had to remember that she wasn't like other women—not anymore— and she didn't have the option of being a wife and mother to fall back on. For her it was a career or nothing.

She needed to keep to her vow. She needed to remember that if she had to leave *this* job, her only option might be working for her sister.

She didn't want to have to start over yet again. The only way she was going to keep this job was to be firm with herself and focus on doing the best she could.

She almost believed herself that she could do it, she could keep her vow—until Henry walked through the door.

"Morning, Astrid. Have you got any messages for me?"

She looked up into his bright blue eyes and forgot what he'd asked. All she could remember was the way his shoulders had felt under her hands last night. The softness of those firm lips of his against hers. And the way he'd twisted his fingers in the back of her hair.

"Astrid?"

"Yes, Henry."

"Messages?" he asked.

She handed him the messages and realized she'd done it again. Allowed her crush to interfere with her professional career.

Henry had taken one look at the button-down suit that Astrid had on and realized that kissing her last night had been a mistake. He knew he had to retreat. Had to give her room to regain the confidence she'd had the day before. He should have known that a woman who'd been badly burned by an office affair wouldn't want to jump into another one with her new boss.

But the moonlight had been too entrancing.... Hell, the moonlight had absolutely nothing to do with why he had kissed her. It had been Astrid—her lips, her body and her sexy smile that had tempted him. That and the fact that he didn't like that Daniel Martin had touched her.

That the other man had at one time claimed Astrid as his own.

He was first and foremost a competitor. The need to win had been burned into the fabric of his being at a very young age. His mother had often blamed Malcolm for the fact that he was so competitive, but she was just as aggressive when it came to her career.

There was a rap on his door.

"Come in."

"Sir, I mean, Henry. Davis from accounting is here to see you."

"Close the door, Astrid," Henry said.

She stepped inside and closed the door behind her. "Yes?"

"Does he have an appointment?"

"No. But he says its urgent. You do have ten minutes if you wanted to see him. Just a reminder—Steph Cordo is due here in twenty minutes and I know you want to be available then."

He smiled to himself. She was very efficient and the best assistant he'd ever had. Okay, the only one, but she was still good.

"Thank you. When Steph gets here, escort her to the conference room. We'll bring in everyone she needs to talk to. Also, Steven will be stopping by toward the end of the hour with her."

"Steven?"

"My half brother. We are going to set up an in-store performance for Steph at the Everest Mega Store located in Leicester Square."

"Sounds good. Do you want me to interrupt if Davis isn't out of here in ten minutes?"

"That'd be great."

She turned to leave, and though he was trying to keep his mind on business, he couldn't help but notice the way her slim-fitting skirt hugged the curves of her backside.

"Henry?"

She paused in the doorway. "After Steph's

appointment, I'd like five minutes of your time."

"What for?"

"We can speak later. I don't want to mess up your schedule."

"Davis can wait. Tell him I'll have time tomorrow morning and then come back in here."

"Really—"

"I've made my mind up."

She left without another word. It was good to be the boss. Since he'd earned the top spot on the team and here at the office, he got things his way. Something that Henry freely admitted he liked.

She reentered his office less than a minute later, closing the door behind her, but remaining in the doorway.

"Sit down."

She did.

"What's on your mind?"

"Last night."

"What about it?"

She took a deep breath and looked him straight in the eye. His respect for her rose a notch.

"I like you, Henry. But this job…I'm aware that this is probably my last chance to make a go at the music industry. And I don't want to mess this up."

"Why would last night have anything to do with that?" he asked. "I'm not your last boss. If I kiss you, I'm not going to fire you."

She glanced down at her lap where her fingers were tightly laced together. "I wasn't fired due to our affair. Daniel kept me on after things ended. I don't want you to get the wrong impression of Daniel."

Henry didn't like her defending the other man. That reaction made little sense to him so he ignored the source. "Why then?"

"I was sick. And I did take a lot of time

off from work. That was what made him sack me."

"Did you find it difficult to work with him after your affair ended?" he asked. Then realized he was prying into very personal areas. He could work with Astrid, kiss her and whatnot, without knowing any of the details of her past. Except he wanted to know more.

"No. It was something else entirely. But I like you and I really like this job. I don't want to make another decision based on lust and end up regretting it."

Henry leaned back in his chair. "So you lust after me?"

"Henry, please, I'm trying to be serious."

"Sorry, Astrid, but you brought up sex and I'm a guy. That means my mind is going to automatically shut down."

She smiled. "You are more than some sex-crazed maniac. That's why I'm talking to you. I know you want to beat your half brothers and

I think we have a chance of doing that, but only if we both concentrate on business."

"This is all in my best interest?" Henry asked.

"Well, it's not going to be bad for me, either," she admitted.

His respect for Astrid rose even more. And he realized she wasn't the kind of woman he'd always been attracted to. She was so forthright. She wasn't just out for herself and what she could get.

That was more refreshing than he would have imagined.

"I just want us both to be successful," she said.

He stood up and walked around to the front of his desk, leaning back against it so that he faced her. "Thank you, Astrid. I will do my best to keep my baser instincts in check, but I'm not sure I'll be successful."

"I'm going to keep dressing in my ultraprofessional suits," she said.

He laughed. It wasn't the clothing or her sexy
body that was making him want her, though
they definitely played a part. It was the woman
she was, but he doubted telling her would help
either of them.

It was a late night almost three weeks into
her tenure at Everest Records. She'd been on
the phone with a number of radio stations
throughout the U.K. and Europe to make sure
that everyone had received the packages she'd
sent out about Steph.

Henry had been out doing his nightly club
thing, and she was sitting in the office by
herself.

"Another late night?"

She looked up to see him standing in the
doorway. "My boss can be a slave driver." She
smiled.

"Really? I thought I was easing up a bit. Giving you room to grow and all that."

"Is that what you are trying to do?"

"I think so. You said that you wanted a career in music so I've been introducing you to all the departments—A & R, marketing.

"It has been smashing," she said.

"Truly?"

"Well, it's different than what I did for Daniel. I mean, for him I was just his assistant, but you are giving me my own responsibilities. I'm enjoying it."

Henry nodded. "Good. Then maybe you can start to relax here at the office."

"I already have," she said. It surprised her. She'd kept her guard up and tried not to see Henry as anything other than her boss. But he was a stand-up guy behind the celebrity profile. She fielded a dozen questions a day from magazines and newspaper reporters about where he was going to be. Some of the information she leaked because Henry wanted some extra coverage for a group or for his friends.

"Good," he said again, leaving her to go into his office. She just sat there and tried not to think too much about the fact that he was treating her like an employee and he hadn't tried to kiss her once since that night at her flat. Which was perfect, really, since she wasn't interested in him as a man. At least that's what she kept telling herself.

Astrid borrowed her sister's car for the evening and left it parked near Waterloo Station so she could have Henry drop her off there if she needed to. She didn't want to risk having him at her flat again. They were hitting another string of clubs tonight. It had been four weeks since she'd talked to him in his office. For the most part he kept his hands to himself. But his gaze often lingered on her lips or her figure.

And she found herself wishing she'd kept her mouth shut. She wanted to feel his arms around her. Each night in her dreams she relived that brief kiss he'd given her at her door. She wasn't going to allow herself to pine for him, but a part of her—the part that she sometimes thought would never come to her senses—longed for Henry.

She took the Underground to Covent Garden and walked to Bungalow 8. The exclusive club had been known to turn away even celebs, so she was a little intimidated to approach the bouncer.

"Can I help you?"

"I'm meeting Henry Devonshire," she said. "I'm Astrid Taylor."

"Of course, Ms. Taylor. He asked that you join him in the VIP area. The hostess will direct you once you are inside."

The electronica music pulsed through her body as she followed the hostess to the VIP area. She should be getting used to so many late nights, but she wasn't. And when she approached Henry's table, she noticed that it was full of people. She'd realized quickly that part of Henry's charm was his easygoing manner.

No wonder the bouncer had simply let her in. She was probably one of fifteen people who'd used Henry's name to get in the door tonight.

He looked up when she approached and gave her a half smile. He gestured for her to have a seat at the end of his table and she sat down next to a man she'd seen on TV and Lonnie from their office. She chatted with the TV guy—"call me Alan"—until he left with a group of three women. Henry waved her down to a seat next to him.

"Have you been listening to this group?"

"Hard not to," she said. Since the music even in the VIP section was blaringly loud, it made conversation impossible.

"What do you think of it?"

She turned her head toward the sound and closed her eyes. One of the first things she'd realized about good music was that it had the power to entrance a person. Make someone forget about the problems of everyday life. The band didn't spark that feeling.

"It's nice."

"But not great," Henry said.

"Exactly. They are a good band and I bet they'd do well for one album, but I don't think they have the kind of sound that would sustain a lasting career," she said.

"Good. I like your instincts."

"Thanks," she said.

"The next band is the one that Roger recommended to me. I think you'll like them."

"Why?" she asked. She wanted to know what Henry thought she'd like and why. Did he really know her? It had only been a few weeks, though she'd come to know him pretty well since they'd spent so much time together?

"Because they have a nice sound with a pop groove but there's something retro about their lyrics. They talk about real emotions, which I've noticed you like as I've been listening to the tapes of the bands you want me to sign."

"I noticed you noticing," she said. Over the past two weeks he had paid a lot of attention to her at work, asking her opinions on bands, giving her decision-making power on booking groups for radio tours and whatnot. Mostly he's treated her like a respected peer, and that was all she'd needed.

"Good. I wanted you to see that I'm not like Daniel," Henry said.

"Why?" she asked.

"Because I'm going to kiss you again, Astrid, and this time I don't want you to run."

She felt foolish when he said it like that. But then she was human, she thought. And resisting temptation, especially the type that he offered, was too hard.

"I'm not going to make another foolish mistake," she said, not sure if she meant the words for Henry or for herself.

"Good," he said. He reached under the table and took her hand in his. His big hand completely engulfed hers. They announced the band XSU. Sounded like some American university band and the guys looked the part.

In their denim jeans and faded vintage T-shirts they looked as though they were meant to be singing to university crowds instead of this very upscale and trendy club in London.

They introduced their first song and the music was…sex-disco. A pulsing beat that made her want to get up and dance. She was tapping her feet and noticed that Henry was moving to the beat, as well. The dance floor, which had been crowded before now, seemed to be a single solid wave of dancing bodies.

Henry used his grip on her hand to tug her to her feet. They were in the middle of the swaying crowd. Henry's body brushed hers often as they danced, each brush reminding her that she'd done a poor job of keeping the distance she'd wanted between them.

She tried to be stiff, tried to keep a part of herself locked away but it was impossible. She wanted Henry. And this music reminded her that life was meant to be lived, not hidden away from.

She stopped thinking she had to be professional and just relaxed, allowing herself to just be herself. And that moment changed her. She looked into Henry's impossibly blue eyes and saw more than she'd thought to see.

In taking the measure of the man, she knew that no matter what happened between them, she'd never regret the time they spent together.

Five

Something had changed in Astrid when XSU had started playing. She seemed to sparkle with life as she moved on the dance floor, and Henry wanted to be the only one who basked in that glow.

He kept one hand on her hip as they danced. Her body brushed against his, teasing him with each rhythmic move she made. He wanted more than those fleeting touches. He wanted her breasts pressed solidly against his chest, his hands holding her hips and that tempting mouth of hers under his.

The music stopped, but he scarcely noticed. The crowd applauded, and in the back of his mind Henry realized that he'd found the first group he'd sign to the Everest Records label, and he'd use a similar path to the one he developed with Steph Cordo. But he'd also found something else, he thought.

Astrid watched him with those big brown eyes of hers, and he leaned in and kissed her. He didn't think about consequences or warnings. Didn't think about winning or business. Just thought that this woman was temptation incarnate and he was tired of denying himself.

He lingered over her mouth. The last three weeks had been too long as far as his body was concerned. Blood flowed heavier through his veins. Her hands came to his shoulders, anchoring her as she rose on tiptoe to deepen their kiss.

The crowd swayed around them as the band moved on to the next song, but Henry felt the world narrow until he and Astrid were alone.

She tasted tangy and sweet and of something that was uniquely Astrid. There was an energy between them, and when he lifted his head she tunneled her fingers into the hair at the nape of his neck and brought their mouths together again.

She sighed as he kissed her. "I've been dying for your kiss."

He took her hand and led her off the dance floor. "Have you?"

She nodded.

"I'm tired of pretending that I don't want you, but that doesn't mean I think this is right. You already guessed that my relationship with Daniel complicated my last job. I can't afford to let that happen again."

"What can I say to change your mind?" Henry asked.

"I'm not sure. I just…I'm not saying I don't want you, just that I'm not sure it's wise for me to get involved with you, Henry."

"We will figure it out," Henry said. "I want to go talk to the band. Want to come with me?"

She nodded.

He held on to her hand and he no longer felt that she was just his assistant. Now he knew she was his. And he liked that. He needed to make love to her before he'd really feel she was his.

The band had a small group of women hanging around them as he approached. Henry used his celebrity to get closer to the band. He approached the black-shirted bouncer protecting the backstage area, who was turning away scantily clad women and overzealous fans.

"I'm Henry Devonshire, and I'd like to speak to the band."

"Henry Devonshire. I saw you score a converted try in the last minute of the London-Irish game—your last one."

"That was a great game. Stan got that penalty and I thought we were going to lose."

"But you didn't. You were brilliant."

"Thanks," Henry said. "I'd appreciate it if you'd let us back to see that band."

"Sure thing, mate." The bouncer stepped aside and let them through.

"Henry Devonshire," he said as he approached the lead singer.

"Angus McNeil," the young man said, shaking Henry's hand.

"I like the sound of your group."

"Thanks, man. We've been experimenting with a lot of different influences and I'm not sure we have it right yet."

"I'd like to talk to you a little more about that. I'm in charge of Everest Records now," Henry said. "Do you guys have a manager?"

"Yes. B&B Management."

"I've never heard of them," Henry said. He glanced over at Astrid to see if she were familiar with the company, but she shook her head.

"It's actually my older brother and one of his mates," Angus said a little sheepishly. "No one wanted to talk to us unless we had a big deal going. So Bryan went to the library and got a few books…. Ah, man, you don't want to hear all that, do you?"

"Yes, we do, Angus," Astrid said, stepping forward. "At Everest Groups, we like to know everything about the artists we sign."

"That's why we are here," Henry said. "Do you have another set or can you guys come with me to talk?"

The other band members had wandered over to their group and milled about exchanging glances. Henry decided he should step away and let them talk.

"Here's my card. I'm going to be out in the club for another hour or so. If you have time to talk tonight, great, if not, no problem. Call tomorrow and we will set up something."

He led Astrid back to the VIP area, but he was restless and didn't want to sit and wait. He ordered drinks for both of them and Astrid put her hand on his.

"I can feel the energy crackling around you. What are you thinking about?"

Henry didn't like to share his most intimate thoughts so he kept silent until he realized that Astrid would give him the distraction he needed. "That you still haven't told me your secrets."

"Well, that will have to wait for another time. A noisy nightclub is no place for an intimate conversation."

"I disagree. This is the perfect place. There's a feel of anonymity to being here. The background noise keeps others from hearing."

She tipped her head to the side and then

leaned forward so that their noses almost touched. "It wouldn't keep you from hearing."

He arched one eyebrow at her. "Good. Tell me your secrets, Astrid."

She shook her head. "Not unless you tell me yours. Not the stuff I can read in *Hello!,* but the real Henry's secrets. Why are you so restless right now?"

Henry didn't want to share that with her. He was reluctant to let anyone know about the impulses that had always driven him—the need for immediacy in every area of his life.

Astrid was still almost high on her new sense of self. She had always let the men in her life… well, Daniel, set the tone and the pace of their relationship. And she knew if she was going to have any chance at making any kind of relationship with Henry work, she needed to change.

Instead of focusing on hiding her own secrets,

she wanted to know about his. What had shaped Henry into the man he was today?

He wrapped his arm around her shoulder and drew her closer to him. "I'm not restless, love. I want to be alone with you so we can finish what we started on the dance floor."

She shivered as he spoke straight into her ear. The warmth of his breath against her neck sent electric pulses flooding through her body. She wanted him, too.

And that scared her. Lust she could deal with but this was more than lust. She liked Henry. Liked the man who was more than his press bio. And she was afraid to trust that gut-deep feeling about Henry. She thought he was different, but there was no guarantee any relationship between the two of them was going to last more than a few months.

"What's that look for?" he asked her.

"I'm scared that I'm in over my head," she said in a moment of candor. She might regret it later, but if she'd learned anything it was not to pull her punches. There was no "safe-route" in any relationship.

"My first year as a professional rugby player I was constantly terrified. My stepdad was the coach and I knew that if I screwed up, he'd come down on me. And I played from a place of fear for the first three games, before one of the guys said to me, 'I heard you were good, but now it looks like that was all bullshit.'"

"That wasn't very nice."

Henry shrugged. "I was giving in to the pressure from every avenue, so I made a decision that I was going to play for myself. Not for Gordon or for the crowd. Just for myself."

"Did that work?" Astrid asked.

"Yes, it did. My playing started improving and eventually I was made captain."

"Good job," she said.

"I used that same theory off the pitch. I live my life on my terms."

"I'm trying to do the same, but there is always a fear—"

"Stop worrying, Astrid."

He glanced over her shoulder and stood to greet someone else—a tall dark-haired young man whose shaggy hair reached his shoulders.

"I'm Bryan Monroe. I represent XSU."

"Glad to meet you. This is Astrid, my assistant. Would you like to sit down and join us for a drink?"

"Love to."

Astrid sank back into her seat and just observed Henry doing his thing. People came and went from his table, which was the norm for Henry, but he kept his attention on everyone. He always had a glass of seltzer water on the table in front of him. She'd quickly realized that her boss didn't drink on these long nights out. And he had a work ethic that would put anyone to shame.

Daniel had often used other people to make things happen. She had observed him leaving clubs early with groupies while his underlings stayed and talked details. Every minute she spent with Henry made her like him a little more.

She started to get tired and fought to keep from yawning at about two in the morning. She signaled to Henry that she was going to leave.

"Wait for me," he said to her.

Thirty minutes later, they walked out of the club together. "I think we're going to get XSU."

"Definitely. Bryan sounded very encouraging. I'll follow up with him first thing tomorrow."

"I'll give you a ride home," Henry said.

"Not necessary. I drove Bethann's car today."

"Why?"

"I didn't want to take advantage of you. I

appreciate the fact that you are always giving me a ride but it seemed important to have my own way home."

"Why is that?" he asked.

"Because I always want to invite you up to my place and that's not a good idea, is it?"

Astrid didn't regret her candor. They both knew the attraction between them was growing. There was nothing they could do about it.

"I think inviting me up is a fine idea. Why haven't you?"

"Because you're my boss, Henry," she said. The night breeze was cool and a little crisp as she tipped her head back to stare up at the stars.

"Why is your name Henry?"

He laughed a soft sound. "It was my mum's dad's name. What about you, Astrid?"

"My mother got it from a book. Bethann was

named after my mum's mum and me...I get a name from a book," she said.

"What book?"

"*Pippi Longstocking*. The author was Astrid Lindgren. My mum said she wanted me to have that passion for life that Pippi always had."

Astrid looked back over at Henry to find him watching her with that unreadable expression of his. She was talking too much, she knew, but she was tired. Physically of course, because her body had yet to adjust to the night owl hours, but also tired of keeping parts of herself from Henry. She wanted him to know the woman she was. Wanted him to look at her and see the real woman.

"I like that. Your mum sounds like she knew what she was doing when she named you," Henry said.

Astrid wasn't certain about that. A part of her had always felt as though she had to live a larger life than her sister. Bethann was driven and always made the right choices. She had achieved more and accomplished great things, as opposed to Astrid, who was always starting over.

"I'm not so sure. But I do like where I am right now," she said.

Henry grabbed her hand, linking their fingers together as they walked down the street to where he'd parked his car.

"Have you ever thought about what you'd name your children?"

Astrid felt a sting of tears at his question. And turned away from him.

"Astrid?"

She shook her head. "Probably after my parents. You?"

"I've always thought I'd name a son after Jonny Wilkinson, the great rugby player."

"Better hope your wife likes the sport," she

said. She tried to keep her tone light, but she knew that children was never going to be an easy topic for her…. How had they taken this track?

Henry didn't want to talk about kids; he'd never really thought much about them other than when his mum had given birth to his two younger half brothers. But there was a tone in Astrid's voice that made him believe he should pursue this line. There was something more to the way she had answered his throwaway question.

"What are your parents' names?" he asked.

"Spencer and Mary," she said. "I really don't want to talk about this. I'm not even sure how we ended up on this topic."

He unlocked the passenger door of his car and helped her inside. He walked around to the driver's side and sat behind the wheel for a minute before starting it.

"My mum contemplated naming me Mick after Mick Jagger, but in the end she said she wanted to name me after the man who always loved her."

"That's sweet," Astrid said. She had to wonder how hard it was on Henry growing up the way he had. "Why did you play rugby? Wouldn't it have been easier for you to try to be a musician?"

Then she covered her mouth with one hand as a thought occurred to her. "Or can't you sing?"

"I can sing," Henry said. "Not very well, but I can sing."

"So why not music?"

"I'm a stubborn cuss," he said, starting the car. "I didn't want anyone to say I had anything given to me. I started playing rugby when I was eight. I'd already grown up in the glare of my mum's spotlight and the infamous circumstances surrounding my birth…. If I achieved anything I wanted it to be on my own terms."

He pulled out and started driving toward Astrid's car. "Where are you parked?"

"Near Waterloo," she said, giving him directions to the location.

"You were very wise to make that choice so young," she said. "Bethann is like that. She's a solicitor. Always knew she wanted to be one."

"What about you?"

"I always knew I wanted to live in London," she said with a little laugh. "I love the excitement of the city and being so close to everything."

"Why don't you live in town?"

"Well, Woking was all I could afford on my own and all my mates are married now. Anyways, that's why I have a flat in Woking."

"I meant how did you find your way to the music industry?" Henry pulled into the car park where she'd left her car.

"My car's in the second level," she said. "I took a job out of university as a receptionist. It was with Mo Rollins Group, and I just sort of worked my way up. The funny thing is the longer I worked there the more at home I felt.

"It's that green Ford Fusion."

He pulled up behind the car and she gathered her bag to get out. But he wasn't ready to say good-night just yet.

"And now you're working for me. Still like this industry?" he asked.

"After a night like tonight? You bet. I loved the raw sound of XSU and once you sign them it'll be exciting to watch their transformation into a solid band."

"I agree. I had thought of being a sports agent or a recruiter."

"Why didn't you? I remember that telly show you had a few years ago that featured child protégés of the sports world."

"You do? Did you watch it?" he asked.

"Sometimes," she admitted. "How did you get into doing that?"

"My mum knows all kinds of people in the entertainment industry and after my injury she started putting me in touch with them."

"She sounds like she's very helpful."

Henry laughed. "She's a meddler. I told her I was going to live off my investments and just party all the time. That motivated her to use every contact she had to get me in touch with someone who could put me to work."

"And she got her way, didn't she?"

"Yes, she did. So I had the show, and I was talking to my own agent from when I was with the London Irish, but it was a frustrating job and I didn't really enjoy it."

"Is that when you turned to music?"

"Yes. I had the contacts in this world." Henry said.

"And it gives you something in common with your mum."

"Yes, it does. Want to come back to my place for a nightcap?"

"Um…what?"

"I don't want this night to end. I don't think you do either," he said.

She hesitated and then sighed. "No, I don't want it to end. But I have a busy day tomorrow."

"I know your boss."

"Yeah, that's what I'm afraid of. It's hard to balance working together with a personal relationship."

"Is it? Everest Group has no policy against fraternization, so your job isn't in jeopardy at all."

"Will that still be true if I say I want to go home?" she asked.

"Of course it will be. I think you know me better than that," Henry said. "And if you don't, then going home is definitely what you should do."

She bit her lower lip. "I'm sorry."

"It's fine. I guess I'll see you at work tomorrow."

"Yeah," she said, climbing out of the car. He watched her walk to her vehicle, and she opened the door, tossing her purse inside before looking back at him.

"Do you really want to pursue a relationship with me?" she asked.

He nodded. He couldn't get her out of his mind and he was tired of trying. He was going to have Astrid Taylor if for no other reason than they might be able to work without the tension of wondering what they'd be like together.

"I'm going to be honest with you, Henry. I'm not sure sleeping with you is in my best interest."

"Well, when you put it that way, I'm not either," Henry said. He reached out and tugged on one of her curls. He didn't want her to say no to him, but he knew that she had a lot more at stake than he did. He was trying to go slowly with her, but he was used to just reaching out and taking what he wanted.

And damn the consequences.

"Come to my country home this weekend," he said. "We can ride horses and play rugby and get to know each other."

She shook her head. "I already have plans."

"Then invite me along," he said. A shy man never got what he wanted.

"It's with my family…. Still want to come?"

"Yes. What's the occasion?"

"My sister's birthday. My mum's having a dinner party for her."

Henry realized that Astrid thought she had taken a risk by inviting him. And he wasn't about to pass it up. "I'd love to."

"Good. I'll see you at work tomorrow, Henry. Thanks for the lift."

"You're welcome. Drive safely, Astrid."

She got in her car, and he backed up to let her leave in front of him. She was completely unlike any other woman he'd ever met and he was beginning to understand that was part of what attracted him to her.

Six

Astrid had had second, third and fourth thoughts about inviting Henry to her parents' house for Bethann's birthday, but she'd asked and he'd accepted, so there was no turning back now.

Henry hadn't been in the office the past two days so she hadn't seen him since she'd invited him. He'd sent her a text message the night before, asking what time to pick her up. Now she was standing in front of the mirror in her bedroom wishing that she'd turn into some-one else. Someone who knew what she was doing with her life instead of a woman who just bumped along.

The bell rang and she sighed.

She walked through the flat and opened the door to find Henry standing there. He wore a striped button-down shirt with an open collar and a pair of dark trousers. He hadn't shaved but the light beard on his jaw made him look even sexier than he normally did.

"Come in," she said, stepping back so he could enter. "I have to grab my bag and then I'll be ready to go."

"Take your time," he said.

She went down the short hall to her bed-room and gathered her stuff as quickly as she could. When she came back Henry stood in front of the wall where she'd hung her family pictures.

"Is this Bethann?"

"Yes. When she passed her A levels. That's my parents' place, as well."

"Everyone looks happy," he said.

"We generally are," she said. She'd taken that happiness for granted. Thought that because she had a sunny outlook, her life would follow that path. But experience had taught her otherwise.

"Ready then?"

"Yes," he said, walking toward her. But instead of continuing on to the door, he stopped and pulled her into his arms.

He kissed her, and she shut her eyes, savoring that moment of closeness. A moment that passed all too quickly as Henry ended the kiss and then put his hand on the small of her back to lead her to the front door. He waited while she double-checked her lock and then they went downstairs.

A neighbor whose name she didn't know snapped a photo of them and then asked to have his picture taken with Henry. This was his life, she thought as she snapped a photo and then returned the camera.

Henry's mobile rang when they were in the car and on the A. He glanced at the caller ID.

"It's my mum. I have to take it."

"No problem," she said.

He put the phone on speaker. "Hello."

"Hi, Henry, it's Mum. Have you had a chance to talk to your friends about the television idea?"

"Yes. They are taking the idea up the chain of command. I think we will hear something soon."

"That's good. What are you doing today?"

"A birthday party for a friend," Henry said.

Astrid liked the respect and affection in his voice as he spoke to his mother. It was clear that their relationship was a close one. She continued to listen in on their conversation until he hung up.

"Sorry about that," he said.

"It's fine. She dotes on you, doesn't she?"

"Too much I think. But for a long time it was just the two of us, and she's never stopped taking care of me."

"That's really sweet. When did she remarry? I think you said you had some half brothers."

Henry talked and drove, weaving effortlessly through the traffic. His car had a powerful engine, and he drove fast but not recklessly. There was that sense of controlled power that she was continuously aware of with him.

"She married Gordon when I was nine. I'd started playing rugby and he was at a tourney we went to. They met there. My mum…she's vivacious. Everyone is entranced by her when they meet her."

"Much like her son," Astrid said.

"I don't know about that. I don't think I'd look nearly as good in her hats," he said very seriously.

"Are you having me on?"

He laughed. "I am. I got a lot of things from my mum."

His Sat Nav with the Mr. T voice directed him off the motorway and toward her childhood home. She started worrying about how her parents would be with Henry.

They thought nothing of delving into someone's past. And Henry…he certainly had had an interesting one. He parked on the street in front of the house, and she reached over to stop him from getting out.

"Yes?"

"Listen, everyone is going to be curious about you. Don't take it personally. They are just that way."

"It's fine. I'm hoping maybe they'll answer a few questions for me."

"What about?"

"You. I've been waiting for you to tell me

your secrets, and I think meeting your family will show me another side of you."

Astrid shook her head. She wasn't ready to tell him all the details of her relationship with Daniel. That she'd gotten pregnant and lost the baby—and her life and her dreams had changed. "I'm nothing special, Henry. I'm just like any other girl from Surrey."

She reached for the handle of the door, but Henry stopped her this time. "You're not like anyone else in the world, Astrid."

There was something in his blue eyes that made her want to believe him. But she was afraid to trust. Afraid to believe in anything that this man had to say. Yet at the same time she was afraid that those barriers wouldn't be enough to protect her. Because no matter what she tried to tell herself, she knew that she was starting to trust him.

That was why she'd invited him here today and why she let him take her hand in his as they walked up to the front door. Bethann answered the door and Astrid realized her older sister wasn't too pleased with her, or her choice of date.

Henry took his a pint of Guinness outside to the deck, where he stood next to Astrid's dad, Spencer. Spence had a thick Cockney accent and a tattoo of a dancing girl on his forearm that he'd picked up while he'd been in the Royal Marines in Japan. He was affable, but a quiet man who was confined to a wheelchair due to complications from diabetes.

He recognized Henry from his playing days, but had immediately confessed that he preferred football to rugby. The conversation was pleasant enough until Astrid's sister Bethann came to join them.

"Can I have a word?" Bethann asked.

"Sure," Henry said.

"Walk with me down to the summerhouse," she said.

It was easy to see that this woman was a solicitor. Astrid was by no means a passive woman, but Bethann was every inch the protective older sister.

When they got to the summerhouse, Bethann took a seat on the red cushion and gestured for him to do the same.

"You look like you're about to bring me up on charges," he said.

"Don't make fun. I'm sorry if you think I'm out of line, but I can't just let you go without saying something."

"Saying what?" he asked.

"My sister isn't someone you should toy with. She has a family who cares about her, and I think you should know that my practice specializes in women's rights."

Henry felt a swell of compassion for Bethann. Clearly she was at least a little aware of the situation with Astrid's previous employer, and Henry could tell that she was struggling to protect her little sister.

"I am so informed. I have no intention of harming your sister, Bethann. I am attracted to her, and if she decided she wants more from me, then there is nothing you can say that will stop me."

"All men say that."

"Even your husband? Did he make a promise to you and break it?" he asked.

He'd met Percy Montrose, Bethann's husband, briefly before the other man had left to run to Tesco for more ice.

"Especially him," she said. "But when he messes up he fixes it. And I want to know if Henry Devonshire is the kind of man who will do the same."

"Is there really anything I can say that would convince you that I'm an upstanding man? You seem to have your mind made up about me."

"I don't. I'm sorry if it seemed that way. It's just—listen, I love my sister and I don't want to see her stuck—"

Henry put his hand on Bethann's shoulder. "Me, either."

She looked at him, her level stare probing and then she sighed. "Okay."

"Henry?" Astrid called.

"In here," he said.

"Percy's back and we are ready to eat," Astrid said.

"Great," Bethann said, stepping around them and heading up toward the house.

"What did she want?"

"Just to make sure I wasn't going to hurt you," Henry said. "Whatever happened with Daniel...there was more than the ending of an affair, wasn't there?"

"I can't...I don't want to talk about that right now, okay?"

Henry saw the distress he'd caused her with

his question. It was the second time he'd seen the sheen of tears in her eyes.

"Let's go up to the house," he said, letting his pursuit lie for the moment.

She put her arm through his as they walked up to the patio, where her mother had set the table. It was a beautiful day, the kind that they'd learned to relish in England since it was so often cloudy or rainy.

But today the weather was nice. Percy was a likable fellow who had a dry wit. He had no problems teasing everyone at the table including Henry. Astrid clearly liked her brother-in-law and flirted in an innocent way with the man.

"Are you a football man like Spencer?" he asked Percy.

"Not at all. In fact, Spencer used to be a big London Irish fan."

"Used to be?"

"Don't get around as good as I used to, so I

miss a lot of games. Watching it on the telly isn't the same," Spencer said, shifting his wheelchair to intercept the conversation.

"No, it's not. Are you managing well with the wheelchair today?"

"Listen to your doctor," Spencer said by way of answer. "I didn't and look where it got me. I'm afraid I'm a bit stubborn. May have passed that trait on to Astrid."

"I have to say I think you have. She definitely knows her own mind," Henry said.

"That she does," Spencer agreed. "But we did love those games. You know my girls tried to get me to a few once I was in this damned chair but it was too much work and it broke my heart seeing them so exhausted from everything that I told them we weren't going anymore."

"Yes, he used to take both of the girls to the games when they were little. I believe that Astrid even had a poster hanging on her side of the bedroom…. Which player was that?" Percy asked.

Astrid flushed and Bethann swatted at her husband. "Enough out of you."

"You had a poster on your wall?" Henry asked.

"It was of you," she said. Everyone at the table was laughing.

"She had a huge crush on you when you first joined the team," Mary said.

"Mum!" Astrid was flushed with color. And for once she was at a loss for words. Here, with the people who knew her best, there were no barriers like the ones she usually kept up.

"Well, Bethann had a crush on Ronan Keating, and she was an adult then."

"He's cute," Bethann said.

"He looks nothing like me," Percy said.

"I am allowed to like men who don't look like you," Bethann said.

"No, you're not," Percy said with a grin.

The conversation continued on in the same vein and Astrid leaned over to him. "Who's your secret crush?"

"Umm...I don't believe I ever had one."

"No Victoria Beckham posters on your wall?"

He shook his head. He had never been much into lusting after unattainable women. He preferred to focus his attention on real women.

"Come on, whom do you like?" Percy said.

Henry reached under the table and took Astrid's hand in his. "Astrid."

"Oh, ho," Percy said. "Trying to show me up?"

"Is it working?" Henry asked.

"Yes!" Bethann said. She smiled at Henry, and he knew that her fears had been placated for the time being.

The afternoon at her parents' had spilled over into evening, and it was after ten when Henry

and she pulled into the parking area at her flat.
Henry had been a good sport all day.

"Thank you," she said, caught in a peaceful
glow. She kept her head resting on the back of
the seat and just turned it to look at him.

"For what?" he asked.

He'd left the car running and the music playing softly in the background. An American
group—the Dave Matthews Band—"Pay for
What You Get." It was a pay-it-forward type
song that made her realize that no matter where
a person was in life, everyone paid the cost for
their actions. It was a song about karma, and
today she felt hers was good.

Today she'd seen that Henry *was* the type of
man she'd thought he was. He blended easily
with her family, even though she knew he
probably could have bought and sold them
many times over. He had fit in, something
that Daniel never had. In fact he'd never even

met her family, although they'd dated for over a year.

"For putting up with my family," she said.

"I like your family. It took me a bit to realize your dad was having me on with liking football."

Astrid smiled. "He's like that. It's a harmless thing."

"I know. I like him. He reminds me of my stepdad."

"In what way?"

"The way he is with you and your sister. The love he has for your mum. I can tell that family is important to Spencer and it is to Gordon, as well."

"Really? I'm going to tell him. My dad will get a kick out of that."

"Is the wheelchair why you stopped going to the rugby matches?" Henry asked.

"Yes," she said. "It's hard for him to get

around and the seats we typically had weren't easy to get to."

They'd tried to go a couple of games but it really had been a struggle. She had noticed that her father got angry at himself for not having the abilities he used to.

"I have a box at Madejski stadium. Do you think your folks would like to join us at a game?"

"I know they would," she said. "Would you really invite them? It's meant for corporate socializing, isn't it?"

"I can use it for whatever I want," Henry said. "I'm the boss."

"You like saying that, don't you?"

"Yes, I do. I'm a leader."

"Always?"

"Yes, except for when I first started playing, I've always been the one in control. The one making sure everyone else got to where they needed to go."

He was good at it. She suspected it was simply his affability that made most people unaware of the core of steel in him. Subtly events and people were moved where he wanted them to be.

Even her?

She told herself she was the one woman who saw him and who knew the truth about the man behind his BBC Channel Four exposé profile. But she wasn't entirely sure.

It hadn't taken her too long to realize that Henry was really good at keeping the spotlight off himself. He had secrets, same as she did, but he kept them hidden.

"Invite me up," he said.

"I was thinking about it."

"Good. I'll get your door."

He was out of the car and around to her side in minutes. She liked that he took the time to open her door for her. It was an old-fashioned but a sign of respect.

"I didn't invite you up," she said, feeling more like herself when he reached for her hand to help her out of the car.

"I know. But you're going to."

She just laughed. He was all things to everyone. Today she'd seen how easily he could charm her taxi-driver father, her solicitor sister and her brother-in-law. "Promise me this is real."

He looked down at her. "What do you mean?"

She took a deep breath. Was she being too needy? Or reading things into this—into him? Was she making him into the man she wanted him to be? "Are you pretending to be what I need you to be?"

"Why would I? I'm not playing games with you," he said.

She wanted to believe. She truly did. She would make herself crazy if she tried to examine every move he made.

She led the way up to her , surprised at how not-weird it felt to have Henry in her place. She took off her shoes because her feet ached after wearing heels all day.

"Would you like something to drink?"

"Coffee would be great," he said.

She went into the kitchen to make it. When she came back out, Henry was thumbing through the stack of CDs that she had in her living room. "I have too many, I keep saying I'm going to get organized...."

"I'm the same way. I like your taste."

"Do you now?"

"Indeed. Do you mind if I put on some music?"

"No, go ahead. I have some biscuits if you'd like something with your coffee," she said.

"I'd love some. I have a bit of a sweet tooth."

"I've noticed."

"Have you?"

"That little jar of sweets on the end of my desk. I must have refilled it at least three times a week since we started working together."

"You've found me out," he said.

"I have. And I intend to know all about you before much longer," she said. Better to know his secrets than let him find out hers. She left him at her CD player and went to pour the coffee for them. She brought it into her sitting room on a tray that had been her grandmother's.

Henry was leaning back on the settee with his eyes closed. She had switched on her iPod with its Bose docking station, and some old-time jazz played in the background. Louis Armstrong with Ella Fitzgerald singing. The playlist was mellow and eclectic.

She sat down next to Henry and he put his arm around her shoulders and drew her close to his side. After a few minutes he tipped her head up. His mouth moved over hers with surety, and this time there was nothing light or short about his kiss.

Seven

"Dance with me," Henry said. He stood up and drew her to her feet and into his arms.

She wrapped her arms around his waist and rested her head against his chest as the song changed, and the sweet mellow sounds of Alan Jackson filled the room. The country music singer had a way of making Astrid cry whenever she listened to his singing, but she really liked the raw emotionality of his music.

As they swayed, Henry sang quietly along

with the music, his deep voice finding the countermelody to Alan Jackson's. And despite what he'd said earlier about not really having any musical talent, she could tell that he did.

She tipped her head to say something to him, but his mouth captured her words, and he kissed her deeply while he moved their bodies in time to the song.

He bit her lower lip lightly as he pulled back. Nibbling kisses trailed against her jaw until his tongue brushed at the spot just under her ear.

"This is what I wanted to do to you when we were in the club on Wednesday. Pull you into my arms and run my hands down your back."

She shivered, loving the intimate sound of the words spoken right into her ear. "Why didn't you?"

"There were too many people around. I didn't think you'd welcome a photo in *Ok!* Of the two of us."

"No, I wouldn't have." She'd had enough of tabloids to last a lifetime.

His hands found the back of her skirt and drew it up her legs. She felt his hand on the back of her thigh as the music changed to Bonnie Raitt, burning in the fire of love. A fire built in her with the brush of his hands against her. His hips moved in time with the music. His erection brushing against her lower stomach and the music combined with Henry's touch seduced away her fears and worries until she was nothing but a bundle of need and want.

And all of it was centered on Henry Devonshire.

She unbuttoned his shirt so she could rub her hands over his chest. He had a light matting of hair and she liked the way it felt against her fingers. She ran her hands over his pecs and then slowly traced her way down his stomach.

His mouth on hers was hot and real. The sting of his five-o'clock stubble against her skin excited her. He found the zipper in the side seam of her dress and lowered it and before the next song came on the stereo, she was down to her ice-blue panties and matching bra. And Henry had on only his pants.

"Let me look at you," he said, stepping back from her.

He drew her arms out from her sides. "You are one sexy woman."

She shook her head. "I'm not of the same caliber as the women you usually date."

"No, you're not. You are sexier because you are real," he said. "Will you dance for me?"

She hesitated. She wanted to turn him on. She wanted to make him so hot that he couldn't wait to get inside of her.

"Yes," she said.

"Good. Stay here," he said. He left her standing in the middle of her sitting room, the light from the side table illuminating them in its soft glow. The scent of the coffee filled the air. He played with the remote until the song changed and a new tune started.

"'Let's Get It On'?" she said with a laugh.

"Yes, baby. Show me you feel like I feel."

She threw her head back and laughed. In this moment she felt so damned alive. Her hips moved unconsciously in time with the rhythm of the music, her gaze on Henry. He leaned back on the settee to watch her, and she felt her inhibitions slowly fall away until she was dancing toward him.

With her hands on the back of the settee, she leaned down to sing softly into his ear while moving her body over his.

"You have a sexy singing voice," he said.

"Do I?"

"Yes. Why didn't you tell me you could sing?"

She perched on his lap. "Because I'm not good like the singers you listen to all day."

"You're better," he said, "because you only sing for me."

His hands came up to her waist and caressed their way up her back. She stood up and took a step away from him, swirling out of his reach, only to realize he'd unfastened her bra. She let it slide down her arms and drop to the floor.

Suddenly, she felt his hands on her back open, stronger now, pulling her close until she was nestled in his arms. His body swayed with the rhythm of hers. His hands cupped her breasts. His hard-on nudged her buttocks, and she felt as if she was going to explode.

He put his mouth on the base of her neck and suckled gently while they danced to the music. She couldn't take much more. She felt achingly empty and tried to turn in his arms. But he held her in place with one big hand on her waist.

The music changed again. This time "Sexual Healing" played, and she couldn't help but shiver as his hands slid lower until his fingers were sliding between her skin and her panties.

She tried to turn and this time he let her. She pulled his head to hers, her mouth devouring his as passion overwhelmed her. She wanted him. She needed him. *Now.*

She walked them backward toward the couch and he followed her lead. She put her hands between them fumbling for his belt, but he stopped her. "Not yet."

"I need you, Henry."

"Soon, baby. But I want you to come first."

She shook her head, but Henry wasn't paying attention to her. He'd lowered his head and was kissing her breast. One hand stroked her and then she felt the warmth of his breath against her nipple.

She tunneled her fingers into his hair, holding him to her breast, needing him to continue sucking on her. Everything in her body reacted to the feel of him. It had been a long time since any man had made her feel the way he did.

"Henry." His name burst from her lips as his other hand slid back between her legs, pushing her panties down her thighs. She moved her legs until the wisp of material slid down to the floor.

Henry stroked her mons and her thighs, with touches that were everywhere, teasing her ceaselessly. Finally his forefinger brushed against her, and she almost screamed with the pleasure of it. But that touch was fleeting. He switched his mouth to her other breast. He rubbed her up and down and then swirled his finger in a light circle.

She did scream then, feeling the beginning of an orgasm ripping through her. She clenched her thighs together and dug her nails into his shoulders.

He lifted his head.

"I like the sound of you coming," he said.

"Almost as sexy as you singing." She'd never seen anything more beautiful than this man in the flush of sexual need for her.

"No more waiting," she said.

"No more," he agreed. He lifted her in his arms and carried her down the hall to her bedroom, setting her gently down in the center of the bed. His clothes were tossed to the floor and he stood next to her completely naked.

She touched his erection, lingering at the tip where a bit of moisture beaded. She swiped her finger over it and brought her finger to her mouth, licking it off.

He growled at the sight. Then he lowered himself until he covered her and they were pressed together, chest to breast, groin to groin. She wrapped her legs around his hips. His mouth ravaged hers. She shifted underneath him, and he rolled over onto his back, drawing her over him.

She'd never been on top. She wasn't sure

what to do and felt so damned exposed, but when he leaned up and took one of her nipples in his mouth, she forgot everything except the sensations he stirred in her.

His mouth found hers. Their tongues tangled, and she felt overwhelmed as his hands roamed all over her body, his fingers rubbing and caressing every inch of her skin while he made love to her with his mouth.

She knelt with one leg on either side of his hips as his hands grabbed her waist. He wrapped his arms around her, and his mouth latched onto her nipple, suckling her strongly.

"Henry!"

Humid warmth pooled in the center of her body and she rocked against him, feeling him against her center. She wanted more. She needed him deep inside her. She needed it now.

This was nothing like the sexual encounters she usually had. It was more intense, more real,

and she forced down the emotions that threatened to surface and focused only on the physical sensations. She wasn't ready to admit that
this was anything more than a physical joining.
She didn't want to start to care for Henry—not
while she knew her secrets were still buried
deep inside.

He was hot, hard and ready between their
bodies. She rocked against him, finding her
own pleasure as he continued to lick and suck
at her breasts. He held her in his strong hands,
to control the movements of her hips.

Skimming his hands down her sides, he ex-
plored every inch of her skin. She felt raw and
vulnerable and wanted to reach for him and
turn the tables, but she couldn't. His hands
and mouth were everywhere, making her crave
more of his touch.

His mouth reached her mons at last and he
rested for a moment, his looking up at her. She

wanted him so badly. Wanted to feel his mouth on her and his tongue and fingers inside her.

"Henry?"

"Hmm," he murmured, turning his head from side to side, caressing her with his entire face.

"Please…"

He moved back up over her body, stretching her arms over her head. She gripped the headboard, wrapping her fingers around the base of it. His strong, rough body brushed over hers in one big caress that brought every one of her senses to hyperawareness. She couldn't take this slow build to passion. She wrapped her legs around his waist and tried to impale herself on him but he pulled back.

He nibbled his way down the center of her body again, pressing her breasts against his face as he continued on his path straight back to her aching center.

She parted her legs, opening them widely for

him, and he lowered his head, taking her in his mouth. First his warm breath caressed her and then his tongue. His fingers teased the opening of her body, circling but not entering her as his tongue tapped out a rhythm against her very center.

She gripped the headboard tighter and tighter as her hips rose and fell trying to force him to penetrate her, but still he held his touch only at the entrance of her body.

"Please, Henry. I need you. Now."

He caught her between his lips and sucked her into his mouth. At the same time he thrust his finger deep into her body. She screamed as her body spasmed. She rocked her hips against his finger and mouth as he kept up the pressure, not letting her come down from her orgasm, but building her up once again.

Henry moved slowly up and over Astrid. He was aching hard and needed a condom fast.

She was languid as she moved against him, her legs tangling with his.

He'd drawn out this lovemaking, because he'd wanted to explore every inch of her passion, find out what it took to turn this woman on. He wanted to know her intimate secrets. And he refused to stop until he knew them all. Tonight was just the tip of the iceberg.

"I don't want to come without you again," Astrid said.

"Me, either. Are you on the Pill?" he asked.

"I won't get pregnant," she said.

"Good, because I don't have a condom," he said.

"You don't?"

"Why would I carry one around?" he asked her.

She just smiled up at him. "I guess you didn't plan this."

"Not at all," he said.

"You make me feel special," she said.

The words were honestly innocent as she wrapped her arms around him rubbing her hands over his skin. He loved the feel of her long cool fingers on him. When she found the sensitive area at the base of his spine, tracing her finger in a small circle, awareness spread through hers in waves, and a shudder went through his entire body.

He drew her hand away from his body and linked their fingers together, tasting her with long slow sweeps of his tongue against her neck and her collarbone. She smelled heavenly...sex and woman...his woman.

Was she his?

He lifted himself away from her, kneeling between her legs. She touched his thigh, the only part of his body she could reach.

Her fingers were cool against his hip. He needed her under him now. The teasing had gone on long enough—now he needed to be inside of her. To claim Astrid as his. Because whatever else happened between them, tonight she was his.

He tumbled her back on the bed. She held his shoulders as he slid up over her. He tested her body to make sure she was still ready for him. He held himself poised at her entrance. Felt her silky legs draw up along his and then fall open. Anticipation made the base of his spine tingle.

She shifted under him. Her shoulders rotated until the tips of her berry-hard nipples brushed against him.

He lowered himself over her, settling into place between her legs. She skimmed her gaze over his body, down to the place where they met.

He looked down at her but her eyes were shut. "Don't close your eyes," he said, wanting her to see this moment when she became his.

He lifted her hips and waited until their eyes met, then slid into her body. She was a tight fit and he eased inch by inch until he was fully seated inside her. She wrapped her legs around his waist, her ankles resting at the small of his back.

She closed her eyes for a minute, her arms tightened around him. He couldn't breathe anyway as he started to move over her, found her mouth with his. She turned her head away from him, kissed his shoulders and his neck, scraped her nails down his back as he thrust slowly, building them both back toward the pinnacle.

He caught her face in his hand, tipped her head back until she was forced to look at him as he rode her. Her eyes widened and he felt something shift within him. He wanted to go so deep that the two of them would never be separated again.

She gasped his name as he increased his pace, feeling his own climax rushing toward him. He changed the angle of his penetration so that he would hit the G-spot inside her body.

Her mouth opened on a scream that was his name as her orgasm rolled through her body. He continued thrusting, driving himself deeper and deeper until he came in a rush, shouting her name.

He wrapped his arms around her, letting his body relax for a moment. He felt the strength in her arms as she hugged him, and he knew he couldn't let this be a mistake. Not just because of the work situation but because this woman meant more to him than he'd realized.

He got out of bed and went into her en suite bathroom. He had to search to find a flannel, then he wet it and brought it back to the bed where Astrid waited. He wiped her tenderly between her legs.

"Stay with me tonight?" she asked.

He couldn't deny her. He got into bed next to her and pulled her into his arms. Astrid was different than every other woman he'd dated, something he'd felt from the beginning, but in this moment he understood why.

He couldn't sleep as he held her. He knew that his life was complicated and he didn't know where Astrid fit into it. He stayed awake all night puzzling over what to do with this woman who was everything he'd ever wanted in a woman and nothing that he knew what to do with. But there were no easy answers where she was concerned.

When the sun started to rise, he rolled her over and under him, making love to her again. He left her dozing to shower and dress and when he came out of the bathroom she was no longer in her bed.

Astrid had wanted nothing more than to stay in bed and wait for Henry, and that scared her. She knew that it had been wrong to sleep with him without telling him all her secrets.

Because he might start thinking that they could have a relationship that would be more than an affair…

And then what would she say? How would she casually bring up the fact that she couldn't have kids? That her one disastrous affair with Daniel had taken a bigger toll on her than she'd admitted?

"Astrid?"

"In here," she said from the kitchen. "I know you take your coffee black, but how do you like your eggs?"

Henry stood in the doorway freshly showered and dressed. Was she really going to fix him breakfast? She felt that she had to because otherwise she just seemed like a big coward for running away from him.

"I like them fried. But you don't have to fix me breakfast."

"Um…are you sure?"

"Yes," he said. "I'll take that coffee, though."

She poured him a cup of coffee. She couldn't sit across the table from him right now. There was too much on her mind. "I need to shower."

"Go ahead," he said. "Do you mind if I stay? I'll take you to breakfast when're done."

She nodded and left the room as quickly as possible. Standing in her own bathroom, she stared at her reflection in the mirror.

The problem with having a secret like hers was there was no outward sign that anything was wrong with her. Any man who saw her would assume she was a normal female with all the required working parts.

She shook her head. She didn't need to worry about that. Henry wasn't a family man—God, that was a lie. He might not have a wife and child of his own, but he was deeply committed to his mother and stepfather and half brothers.

She showered and quickly got dressed,

thinking the sooner they got out of her flat the better.

"Do you mind working today?" Henry asked, as they left the building.

"Not at all." That would be a lifesaver, she thought. Hopefully it would bring an end to her thoughts and let her get back to normal footing with him.

"Great. Steph is in the studio and I think she needs some direction."

"I'd love to hear her tracks. I'm sure they are really good."

"She gets nervous in the studio. She likes having an audience and without one she kind of shuts down."

Henry drove them to the studios that Steph was using in East London. When they got there, everyone was bustling around, and Henry moved off to talk to Steph.

Astrid stood to the side, feeling as though she didn't fit in. She had worked in the music industry for years but she'd never sat in on a session with an artist. Daniel had said she'd just be in the way and now she realized she was. There wasn't anything for her to do but sit in the corner and sip her coffee.

Henry was in his element, though, and she saw now that he had a gift when it came to saying the right things. Before long Steph was singing, and the sounds were better than her live shows.

She wondered if Henry just intuitively knew what to say to all women. Were the things he'd said last night just lines? Had she fallen for a man who was willing to say whatever he had to to get results?

Fallen? Was she starting to care about Henry? She knew the answer was yes. She realized now that had happened the minute he'd kissed her at her flat the first night he'd taken her home.

The recording studio wasn't too crowded— the only people there were Steph's manager and her mother, who Astrid took a few minutes to chat with. In the control booth were Conan McNeil and Tomas Jimenez, the producer and the sound mixer for this project.

Tomas had been going through a rough patch lately, with his wife leaving him for another man. Unfortunately Tomas hadn't been leaving his problems at the door and Astrid heard the sound of raised voices and saw that Conan was arguing with Tomas.

Henry stepped over to get in the mix and Astrid followed, wanting to make sure things didn't get out of hand.

"If you are too drunk to operate a mixing board then you need to go home," she heard Henry say from across the room.

Astrid walked over to him. He was definitely mad and not afraid to show his temper. "Tomas needs a cab."

"I will call one for him," Astrid said.

Tomas glared at Henry. "You can't make me go home."

"You're right, I can't. But I *can* make sure you don't work until you clean up your act. Astrid, escort him out to the lobby."

She nodded and took Tomas by the arm, but he jerked away from her. His arms were swinging as he turned to confront Henry, and he hit her in the chest. The blow was solid and knocked her back against the wall where she hit her head.

"Ouch!"

Henry advanced on Tomas, his anger evident on his face.

"I'm sorry. I didn't mean to hit her," Tomas said, backing away.

"Out!" Henry pointed to the door and Tomas left without another word.

"Are you okay?" Henry asked, coming to her side.

"Fine. My head is a little sore, but I'm fine."

Henry hugged her close for a second but stepped away as soon as the door to the sound booth opened again and Duncan, one of Henry's producers, walked in.

As he went to talk to the man, she wondered if Henry was hiding his relationship with her. She hoped not. She'd been Daniel's secret lover and that had ended horribly. She didn't want to make the same mistakes with Henry.

<u>Eight</u>

Astrid stopped in the corner shop on her way to work for some headache tablets. All the late nights she'd been keeping with Henry were causing her to lose sleep. She smiled at Ahmed as she entered. He'd been running this shop since she moved here, and he always greeted her warmly.

"You are getting famous," Ahmed said. "Will you still shop here for much longer?"

She shook her head. "Stop being funny. I'm

not famous and you are my favorite corner store."

She picked up a bottle of water, and as she went to the front to get her headache tablets, she saw on the cover of *Hello!* magazine a photo of her and Henry. She blanched at the image of the two of them on their first night working together when he had leaned in to kiss her.

"I…I'll take a copy of this."

She paid for her water and the magazine and walked out of the shop quickly. As she got on the above-ground commuter train, she felt that people were staring at her. She hated this. This feeling of being in the tabloids again. She'd been in them before—just a brief mention of the faceless girl—the latest tart to grace the bed of Mo Rollins's number-one producer. At least with the situation with Daniel and the Mo Rollins Group, her photo hadn't been in the papers.

She opened the magazine and saw that the photo was captioned simply: Latest bird to land in hot, hot, hot Devonshire bastard's love nest.

Ugh! That was horrible and made her sound like…like some sort of short-term affair for Henry. Which she might be. She had her secrets and presumable he had his.

But they'd also spent lots of time together, and she was coming to know him, the man behind the celebrity. He's had dinner with her at Bethann and Percy's house, and she'd met his half brothers twice when they'd come to the office to celebrate the milestones that Henry was making with Everest record Group.

Steph's first single release from their label was climbing the charts. She was in demand on all the talk shows in the U.K. and throughout Europe, and her performance on Graham Norton had caught the eye of an American concert promoter who wanted her to do a small tour of House of Blues venues in the States.

Henry had included her in everything with Steph, which made her feel part of the team. Things were going well professionally for both of them. But now, looking at this…

Her cell rang and she glanced down to see who was calling—Bethann.

"Hello, Bethann," she said as she answered the phone.

"Astrid, have you seen *Hello!*?"

"Just this morning. I don't—"

"Don't what? Know how to explain that you are his love bird? Do you want me to sue them?"

"No, Bethann. Thank you for the thought but I think it might be better for me to simply go with the flow here."

"Mum is not going to be happy."

Astrid doubted her mum would care either way. She suspected it was more her own friends that he sister cared about. "Bethann, am I embarrassing you?"

"Don't be ridiculous. I'm worried about you. How could you think otherwise?"

"Because the photo isn't that bad. And being with Henry means having pictures of myself in the mags sometimes." As she tried to reassure her sister, she realized what she was saying was true. If she was going to have a relationship with Henry, then this was going to be part of it.

That also meant she needed to be ready to tell Henry everything, and once she did that… well, then he'd have to decide if he still wanted to be with her. Because she knew that if she didn't tell him, the media would eventually ferret out the truth.

"I've got to go, Bethann. We can talk later."

"Okay." Her sister sounded reluctant, but she gave in to the conversation's end. "Be careful. Love you."

"Love you, too."

Astrid hung up the phone and just sat there waiting for her stop. She didn't know what she was going to say to Henry about all of this.

Her headache was back with a vengeance and she'd forgotten the tablets at the store. She shook her head. It was going to be one of those Mondays.

Henry's cell phone rang just as he finished working out at the gym. He glanced at the caller ID and saw that it was Edmond—Malcolm's solicitor. He debated half a second before answering the call.

"Devonshire," Henry said by way of greeting.

"It's Edmond. Do you have time to meet with me this morning?"

"I'm not sure. Why don't you give my assistant a call and she can set something up?"

"I'd like to speak to you away from the office.

It's about the morality clause that Malcolm has established."

Henry wasn't too concerned about that. He hadn't done anything morally wrong and he knew it. "If you insist. There is a coffee shop here at my gym. I can meet you there in twenty minutes."

"I will see you then."

Henry showered and changed and then called his office.

"Everest Record Group, Henry Devonshire's office."

Just hearing Astrid's voice made him smile. He knew there was still so much of her that was clouded in mystery, but he was slowly getting to know her.

"It's Henry. I'm running late at the gym this morning. Is there anything pressing?"

"Well I spoke to Geoff. He and Steven want to meet here today for the weekly update meeting. I've pulled the financials and we are way ahead of last year's numbers. So that's good news for you."

"Yes, it is. I might beat them." Henry said.

"I'm sure you will."

"We will. And when we do, everyone on the team will be responsible for our success. Anything else?"

She paused and he heard the rustling of papers. "Well…there is a photo of you and me in *Hello!*."

"What are we doing?"

"Kissing. That night you dropped me off at home. The first day I worked for you."

"What can I say, I'm cheeky." He couldn't tell if she was upset by it or not. Was this what Edmond wanted to talk to him about? "Should I apologize?"

"No. Don't be silly. Paparazzi are a part of your life."

"But they aren't a part of yours," he said.

"No. But it's not so bad that I want to run away...yet."

"Yet? I'll have to make sure you don't change your mind."

"Am I that important to you?" she asked.

His phone beeped, indicating an incoming call, and he hesitated for a second. He couldn't tell Astrid that he was falling for her. That when he was with her he found a measure of peace that he hadn't experienced since he'd first stood on a rugby pitch and realized he was good at something on his own.

"I think you know the answer to that," he said, which he knew was no answer at all. "I have to go now. I've got another call."

"All right. Goodbye then."

He hung up, feeling like a jerk, but there was no stopping that. Astrid was complicating his life in numerous ways, and each day they spent together he wanted to extend into another one. But that was dangerous because he'd made a promise to himself to never depend on anyone. To be a part of the team but to keep himself safely insulated from actually getting too close.

Distracted, he clicked over to the other call without looking at the ID.

"Devonshire."

"Henry, it's mum. Why haven't you brought this girl you are seeing to meet us?"

Henry didn't normally bring women to meet his Mum and said as much to her.

"Well, she looks different that your normal type of woman, and I thought maybe she actually was different. Is she?"

"I don't know," he said, being honest with his mum and himself. "She's my assistant."

"Isn't that a conflict of interest?"

"No. Her job isn't threatened at all."

"Henry Devonshire, it's different for a man. Malcolm never said he'd stop producing my records when we broke things off—it was me.

I couldn't stand to see him once we were no longer together."

"Mum, this is different."

"I'm sure you are telling yourself that. If you care at all for this girl then decide if she's different enough that you want her to meet your family. If she isn't, end it now so she can get on with her life."

His mum hung up and Henry stared at the phone. He hadn't thought of their affair in terms of how it would affect Astrid and her career. And from the beginning she'd said her career was important to her.

He left the locker room and went to the coffee shop to meet Edmond. When they'd spoken on the phone, Edmond had mentioned that fact that he would rather discuss this in person than on the phone in the office where they might be interrupted.

Henry had assumed that meant the other man didn't want Astrid walking in on them as assistants sometimes could. They'd agreed on this coffee shop because it was in the building where Edmond had his office. The older man was already there and stood up to shake his hand.

"How's Malcolm doing?"

"Some days are better than others, Henry," Edmond said. "I'd be happy to check and see if he'd welcome a visit from you."

Henry shook his head. "I can't right now. I'm busy with making Everest Records the top performer at the Everest Group."

"You certainly are. Malcolm and I are impressed with the progress you've made. That is why I am here this morning. I would hate to see you lose the competition because of some woman."

Henry didn't like hearing Astrid referred to as *some woman*. "Astrid isn't just some girl I'm shagging."

"I'm glad to hear that, as I'm sure that

Malcolm will be, too. Just be careful that nothing more risqué than this kiss ends up in the papers."

"Is Malcolm recovering?" Henry asked.

"He had his good days and his bad days," Edmond said. "I can't say more than that."

Henry nodded and checked his watch. "I have to go." They stood and the two men walked toward the door. "Does Malcolm ever regret not marrying?"

"I don't know, sir. I've never broached the subject with him."

Henry turned to go, but Edmond stopped him with a hand on his arm. "I think he regrets that you and your brothers are strangers. That you don't know him or each other very well."

Henry nodded and walked away. He tried not to let any of that matter, but deep inside he was glad to hear that Malcolm had regrets. It made him seem more human.

When he entered his office, he saw that

Astrid was on the phone. She looked up at him and smiled and he knew then that he had to choose just as his mum had said. Was he going to try for more permanency with her or should he let her go?

He'd invite her to a rugby match with his stepfather's team. Get the entire family—even those half brothers of his—involved and see how the day went.

There were a swarm of paps outside of Madejski Stadium as Henry and Astrid arrived. He parked his Aston Martin DB-5 and walked with a genial smile toward the stadium. He kept a hold on her hand and lead her through the crowd.

"Henry, who's your girl?"

"What are the details of Malcolm Devonshire's will?"

"Do you have any details on Lynn Grandings's health?"

"When will the other Devonshire heirs arrive?"

Henry waved and moved past the photographers and reporters who called questions to them. Astrid didn't really like the glare of the spotlight that followed Henry around.

Their working relationship continued to be strong the last three weeks and their nights... well, she blushed just thinking about them. With Henry she'd finally realized her sexual potential, she thought. He made love to her all the time and she'd come to find that she needed his touch as much as he needed hers.

"That wasn't too bad," Henry said. "I suppose they couldn't resist a chance to get a photo of Geoff, Steven and me all together."

"It would probably be worth a fortune if I sold it to *Hello!*. I brought my camera to try to get in on the action," she said.

"I bet," he said. "Would you do it? Sell a picture for the money?"

"No, I was teasing. I did bring my camera, though."

"Why?"

They had entered the stadium. "I thought my dad would snap a few photos. You said we'd get to meet the coach."

"And you will. Want to meet the team?"

"Of course. I've already met my favorite player," she said, leaning up to kiss him.

Henry wrapped an arm around her waist, deepening the kiss.

"Very nice," a droll female voice said.

Henry lifted his head and they turned to see a tall brunette. Whose full, pouty lips would put Angelina Jolie's to shame. Astrid had no idea who the woman was, but Henry obviously knew her. There was a tension between the two of them that even she could sense.

"Kaye," Henry said.

"Got a minute?"

"No, actually I don't. I'm hosting a group upstairs."

Astrid was a bit relieved that Henry didn't give in to her request. But a part of her hated the feeling of jealousy that rose in her. Henry and she didn't have that kind of relationship. Daniel had seen other women while he'd dated her. She's thought Henry was different.

"Kaye, this is Astrid Taylor, Astrid, this is Kaye Allen."

Kaye Allen was one of those supermodels Henry had dated. One of the women he'd told her she was sexier than. But standing next to Kaye, Astrid felt wanting.

"I'll head up and take care of the details," Astrid said.

"I'll come with you. Good day, Kaye."

Kaye nodded at them and Henry led the way farther into the stadium and up to the Royal Suite, which they had booked for today's match. Her parents wouldn't be the only guests,

Henry's half brothers by Malcolm Devonshire would also be there, as well as XSU, who were providing an opening show before the match. It was their first professional gig.

Next week they'd be performing at the Everest Mega Store in London at a big event.

For the moment they were alone in the spacious suite with just one member of the catering staff. One long table had been set and several rounds of eight were spaced out.

"Sorry about that," Henry said.

"No problem. So that's Kaye Allen. She's very pretty."

"Yes she is. She's also very clingy."

Astrid wanted to ask more questions, but she'd been described the same way by Daniel at one time and she sensed the baggage hidden in that phrase. "Want to talk about it?"

"No, Astrid. I have no wish to discuss my ex-lover with you," Henry said.

She drew back at his sharp tone. "I was being nice. I don't want to talk about her, either."

It wasn't the first time she'd seen his temper. But it was the first time she'd seen it directed at her. He couldn't talk to her like that.

She walked to the window and stared down at the rugby pitch. The stadium started to fill with fans. Henry came up behind her and offered her a glass of champagne. He put his arm around her shoulder as she accepted the glass.

"I'm sorry. Kaye is...she's never accepted that things are over. And I never should have let my reaction to her upset you."

She turned to look at him. "It's okay."

"Cheers."

She clinked her glass against his.

She wanted to ask more questions, but knew better than to do that. Henry was careful to keep his secrets hidden, and Kaye seemed to be one of his. If she told him everything about

Daniel, she'd have the right to ask him deeper questions. He kept his arm around her and chatted lightly about each player as they came on the field. Kaye's presence had changed the mood between them. Astrid knew he was trying to get them back to the mood they'd been in before running into that woman downstairs, but it was hard for her. For the first time she'd realized that Henry wasn't Mr. Congeniality, as he always appeared to be.

She wondered what else lurked beneath the surface he presented, realizing that no matter how well she thought she'd gotten to know him, he still had secrets that he hadn't shared with her.

"What are you thinking?" Henry asked.

She took a sip of her champagne. She needed to be on her A-game today and not mired in doubt about herself and her position with Henry. Even if she couldn't be the woman who'd keep him happy for the rest of his life.

Because someday Henry would want a family and kids of his own, and that was one thing she couldn't give him. But today she needed to be that girl.

She smiled, but it felt forced even to her. "Just excited about the upcoming match."

Nine

Henry couldn't relax as the afternoon match got started, though he enjoyed the company of Geoff and Steven. They'd each brought a date with them, and Henry, remembering the paps' question about Lynn, wondered what was going on with Steven's mum. This was the first time the three of them had appeared in public together.

Steven seemed in good spirits, though, and they talked at length about the plans to feature

every new artist they signed in the stores—
how they would have little live concerts there.

"Malcolm used to do that when he first opened the Mega Stores," Steven said. "But he got out of the habit in the nineties when he started focusing on his own pursuits instead of the company's. I think the three of us can bring the focus back to the core company values of satisfying our customers, caring about our community and creating synergy between our business units."

"I agree," Henry said.

"We're painting the side of the Airbus planes with the album art from Steph Cordo," Geoff said. "We've actually had a lot of positive comments due to that."

"Perfect," Henry said. He actually liked these men, his brothers. Over the past few months, they had found that they really had a lot in common. It was more than a business drive to succeed. It was something deeper, something he couldn't define.

Astrid glanced over at their table from where she was seated with the members of XSU. The room was like any other VIP room at an event. It was filled with sports stars, celebs and family. She was going to bring them over when he signaled her. And he was comfortable knowing she'd do what he needed her to.

She'd turned into a valuable asset to his work life. And he'd been very careful to keep their relationship private, though open. He didn't want Astrid to feel as though she was sneaking around with him.

And unlike Kaye Allen, whom they'd met earlier, Astrid didn't have any ghosts in her closet. Just a nice family and one ill-timed affair.

He nodded at Astrid, and a few minutes later the group got up and came over to their table. Angus, the lead singer, had met Steven before at the store and before long Henry had the conversation going around the table. He stepped away to see to his other guests. He wouldn't have thought being a record company executive was something he'd want to do, but it had been a challenge he enjoyed. And he was glad to have had it.

"It's going well," Astrid said. "I thought my mum was going to die when you introduced her to Geoff. She thinks his mum is one classy lady."

Henry smiled at Astrid. She kept him real, he thought. It would be easy to look around and see himself as the architect for success at the Everest Group, and he was that, but he was also helping many people make connections that would help them to be happier.

Geoff's younger half sisters were dropping by an after party he was hosting at a local club in the hopes of meeting his mother. And hearing Steph Cordo perform. Her first single was climbing the charts…. There was more here than business. For the first time in his life, he felt connected to people in a good way.

It was odd, because he'd always basically been a loner, even though he'd surrounded himself with mates.

"I'm glad she enjoyed it. Spencer enjoyed his tour of the locker room?"

"Yes, he did. I took a dozen pictures of him in there."

Henry smiled. She had kept her digital camera out most of the time and after seeing that wall of photos in her flat, he knew that Astrid liked to document her life. She took photos of everyone and everything.

Henry watched Astrid take photos of every-one but him. He shouldn't have snapped at her the way he had. It was just that Kaye was one of those women from his past whom he would never have invited to this kind of event. An

event where his family was present. And he
hadn't wanted her to meet Astrid.

He didn't want Astrid sullied by anything
from his past relationships. Okay, he thought,
not going there today. He cornered her, but she
turned to walk away again.

Taking her arm and drawing her close to
him, he turned his back to the room so no one
could see their faces.

"I'm not mad anymore," he said.

"Good for you. I am."

"Astrid—"

"Don't, Henry. I'm sure you'll have some
charming line about why I shouldn't stay mad
at you, and I might buy it. But I'll know deep
inside that you treated me like your assistant
today, and I know that's what I am, but you
invited me to this event as your date."

"I did. And I'm sorry, Astrid. I never wanted
you to have to meet the women from my past.
You are different to me."

"Am I?"

He nodded.

"How?"

"You are the first woman I've brought to meet my family," he said and then kissed her before she could ask him any more questions.

"Henry, come over here." Geoff was waving him over and he glanced down at Astrid.

"Are we okay now?"

"Yes," she said.

"Wait." She wrapped an arm around his waist, extended her arm and snapped a quick photo of the two of them. She wasn't a professional photographer, but her photos were usually very good.

"I want to get a picture of you and your brothers."

"To sell?" he asked with a wink.

"No," she said. "For you. You said you didn't have one."

He had mentioned that to her—though the

media had always linked them, they had never all been photographed together.

"The Devonshire heirs," Astrid said. "I'd like a photo."

The men were good-natured about it, and she snapped a photo of just the three of them. Then of them with the band. And as the afternoon progressed, Henry realized that he had the seeds of a life he didn't want to let go. He wanted to find a way to keep Astrid by his side. To keep these relationships with his brothers going and to continue to build the success he'd found at Everest Group. And he thought Astrid was the key to that.

They all watched the game as it heated up. There was a flat screen on the back wall, but most of the occupants of the suite preferred to watch the action on the field and not on the screen.

Josh and Lucas came up to the suite during

a break in the game. Henry smiled at his two younger brothers as they walked into the room. Astrid snapped a picture of the boys and then went over to talk to them.

It was her first time meeting them, but soon she was laughing and chatting with the teenage boys as if she'd known them forever. It was something she did effortlessly. He realized she made everyone feel at ease. He'd seen it with Roger and others that came through their office. Something that he took advantage of at work.

"Henry, Mum wants you to bring Astrid down to the field after the game," Joshua said. He was the older of the two boys by only eighteen months.

"She does? Why?"

Lucas joined them. "Because she can't get up here to meet her until after she finished talking to the press with Dad."

Both of the boys looked a lot like Gordon except for the eyes, which, like his, were the bright blue of their mum's.

"Mum can meet her at the party later—when she meets Geoff and Steven."

"She's not sure she wants to meet your other brothers," Lucas said.

Henry nodded. The boys didn't have to say anything else. He knew how his mum felt about Malcolm and the proof of his affairs.

"I'll do what I can," Henry said.

"About what?" Astrid asked as she joined him.

"Mum wants to meet you," Joshua said.

"Then let's go," Astrid said, linking her arm through those of his little brothers. "You stay here and keep your party going. I'll be right back."

He watched her walk away and realized he was falling in love with Astrid.

* * *

"Hello, Astrid, I'm Tiffany Malone—Henry's mother."

Tiffany Malone was everything that Astrid expected her to be. She exuded a kind of larger-than-life presence, but Astrid felt some genuine kindness as Tiffany hugged her close.

"Josh and Lucas have been telling me all about your family. Your father is apparently an expert when it comes to the history of this club," Tiffany said.

"Yes, he is," Astrid admitted. "He was beyond thrilled to be here today."

Her parents had gone home early due to her father's getting tired.

"Gordon? Come on over here and meet Astrid."

Gordon wore an open-collar shirt and sport coat over his khaki pants. There was a casual elegance to his style that Astrid saw reflected in a lot of the clothes that Henry wore.

He shook her hand and Henry drifted over to talk to the three of them. As Astrid stood there talking with Henry and his parents, she realized that she was seeing a very intimate glimpse into the private lives of these people.

Astrid was glad to finally be home after the long day they had. Henry had dropped her off first and then went to take his younger brothers home. He'd said he'd try to get back and she hoped he did. Today had been an interesting day.

She'd been worried when they had run into Kaye. She still didn't know the details of that relationship, but she was willing to let it be. After all, she didn't want to tell Henry about Daniel.

Though to be honest, she needed to. Daniel was nothing in her life now. Since she'd been with Henry, she'd come to feel that he was everything to her. Everything she wanted in a man and a lover. He'd pushed her expectations of what a relationship could be and made her realize that girlish fantasies had no place in her life anymore.

She washed her face and changed out of her party clothes into a French negligee that Henry had given her last week. She liked the way the soft silky material felt against her skin. But she also liked the fact that he'd purchased it for her.

He was always giving her little gifts, and she cherished each one of them because they meant that he thought of her during the day and whenever they were apart.

She poured herself a glass of wine to help her wind down after the day and plugged her digital camera into her laptop. A few moments later her photo program opened up and the pictures she'd taken during the day started flashing on the screen as they downloaded.

She smiled as she noted she got a few really

good pictures of Henry. His earnestness as he talked to his half brothers came through and he was by turns, doting when he talked to his younger brothers and very confident as he talked to XSU.

He was everything to everyone, she thought. And to her he was quickly becoming the man she didn't want to live without.

Her phone rang and she glanced at the caller ID before answering. It was a blocked number, but she knew that Henry's number came up like that.

"Hello."

"Hey, baby. Are you still up?" Henry asked.

"I am. Are you coming back here?" she asked.

"I'd like to."

"Good. How long until you get here?" she asked. She'd almost asked him how long until he got *home*. But they didn't have a home to-gether, which hadn't bothered her until this moment. Henry spent more nights at her place than she did at his, but he hadn't mentioned moving their relationship beyond this.

"Twenty minutes, maybe less."

"I enjoyed meeting your family today," she said, trying not to dwell on the fact that, despite her feelings for Henry, she was still probably just a casual affair. Her experience…her past relationships made her reluctant to push for more. What if she wanted their relationship to be more only to find he was content to let things ride?

She couldn't bear to have the dynamic of their relationship change too much. She needed Henry. Needed him to stay the man he was so she could stay the woman she was becoming. A woman who no longer felt shattered and less than other women. Henry made her believe she was worth being with—even if she couldn't get pregnant.

She felt as though finally she was maturing into the woman she'd be for the rest of her life.

"My brothers are in love with you," Henry said, interrupting her thoughts.

That surprised her. "Which ones?"

He laughed. "Joshua and Lucas. They talked about you from the moment we dropped you off until I left my mum's place."

"They are really cute kids. They'd surely cringe if they heard me call them that. But I like them," she said.

And she had. The teens were funny and smart. They didn't act like Henry was a celeb but treated him like their big brother.

"They are good kids. I'm proud to call them my brothers."

"What about Geoff and Steven? You seemed to be getting on well with them today."

She heard the signal of his blinkers in the background as he turned. "I did. It's always different with the three of us because we have so much between us but we are strangers… well, we were strangers. I'm starting to get to know them."

"Geoff is really reserved, isn't he?"

"Yes. But he lightens up the better he gets to know you. Steven's pretty funny, which to be honest always surprises me," Henry said.

"I know. He is scarily smart. I overheard him talking to Percy about quantum physics."

"He is smart. I think that the three of us are a big reflection of the women who raised us."

"In what way?"

"Well, my own mother made sure all her sons cared about each other. We were all family—even Gordon and me."

"I'd agree with that. But there is a definite quality from Malcolm, as well. At least if the rumors about him are to be believed."

"What quality?"

"That charm. All three of you have an easy

way about you when it comes to the opposite sex."

"Do we? Were you flirting with my brothers?" Henry asked.

Astrid smiled to herself. "No. There's only one Devonshire heir I'm interested in."

"That's what I like to hear. I'm parking the car and I'll be right up."

She disconnected the call and a minute later Henry was at her door. He took one look at the negligee she wore and lifted her in his arms and carried her back to the bedroom where he made love to her. Afterward, he held her in his arms and she rested her head on his chest right over his heart hoping that this was where she'd spend the rest of her nights.

Ten

Edmond showed up on Monday at the Everest Records office. Henry wasn't too pleased to see the other man, because Edmond to him always represented Malcolm's absence in his life.

"Is Malcolm okay?" he asked.

"Yes, he's fine. He has asked me to check up on you and your brothers face-to-face to see how things are progressing."

"Then you've seen the report I sent on the

groups we've signed and our projections on how well they will sell."

"Yes, we received it. I hear you were at Madejski with your brothers this weekend."

Henry leaned back in his chair. What was the point of Edmond's visit? Was he here to warn him about Astrid again? He didn't want to be curt to the older man—Henry was aware that Edmond was Malcolm's eyes and ears. Whatever he said to Edmond would make its way back to Malcolm.

"We did. I prefer you call Geoff and Steven the other heirs. We weren't raised as brothers."

"That always pained your father," Edmond said.

Henry shook his head. "How can you say that with a straight face? Malcolm barely knew we were alive."

"That's not true," Edmond said. "But you have your version of your life."

"Tell me one time...*one thing* that Malcolm did for me or Geoff or Steven."

Edmond stood up and walked over to the plate glass windows looking down on the Thames. "He attended your rugby matches when you played with the London Irish."

"Bullshit," Henry said. "I think I would have known if he was there. The media would have gone crazy like they did when he attended Geoff's polo match."

"They were nuts about that, weren't they?" Edmond said. "We learned our lesson on that outing. After that Malcolm learned to be more circumspect when he attended functions for you boys. It wasn't easy for him. He's not a man given to that type of behavior."

Henry approached Edmond, laying a hand on the other man's forearm.

"Why are you here?"

"To check up on you. There was another

photo in *Ok!* of you and that girl. Do you need our help in dealing with her?"

Henry shook his head. "I haven't needed you or Malcolm my entire life. Why would I need you now?"

"You might benefit from the experience he has."

Henry shook his head. "I know how to end relationships and this one with Astrid is fine."

Malcolm's advice might have been helpful when it came to business when he'd first started here, but he'd found his own way. Which Henry acknowledged was the way he preferred to work. He always had. He liked doing things his own way.

"I think Malcolm should stick to business in his communications with me. We are launching one of our artist's newest CD this afternoon at the Everest Mega Store. You might want to stop by there so you can see how I'm running things."

Edmond turned toward Henry. "Fine."

"I can't tell you how relieved I am," Henry said, then realized he was letting his own feelings of resentment toward Malcolm get the better of him. "I'd never deny a child of mine."

"Malcolm didn't either."

"We'll have to disagree on that. I'm glad you stopped by. If you need anything else, my assistant will take care of it for you."

Edmond nodded. "Good day, Henry."

"Good day."

Edmond left and Astrid came into his office. She closed the door behind her. She smiled at him. "Is everything okay? Isn't Edmond Malcolm's right-hand man?"

"He is. Everything's fine. Malcolm just sends Edmond out to check up on me—something he hasn't done since I was a kid."

Astrid walked behind his desk and leaned

back against it. He had sat back down in his executive chair so he turned to face her.

"There's a note in your voice," she said. He snagged her waist and drew her to his lap. "Why don't you like Edmond?"

His arms tightened around Astrid and he drew her close. just let her presence soothe those long-ago feelings of resentment Edmond always stirred up.

"Edmond is fine. I don't like that he is always standing in for Malcolm. *Gordon* is more of a father to me than Malcolm was, and I know that's the way that some men are. But every time I see Edmond, it just reminds me of all the times Malcolm wasn't there."

"I'm sorry," she said.

"It's okay," he said. "I know it sounds like I'm complaining, but I'm not. I always wished he'd just stay out of my life for good instead of dancing around on the fringes."

"Why didn't he?"

"Who knows," Henry said. If Edmond was right and Malcolm had attended his rugby matches, then there was more to the enigma of Malcolm Devonshire than Henry had previously suspected.

"Is everything on schedule for this afternoon?" he asked.

"Yes," she said, trying to stand up, but he held her close and claimed the kiss he'd been wanting since she walked into his office.

He was quickly realizing that having an affair with his assistant was very distracting. Astrid was temptation incarnate. No matter how many times he had her, no matter how often he felt her silky legs around his hips, he always wanted her again. He craved her.

He let his hand caress her body as he deepened their kiss.

"I want to lift you onto my desk and take your panties off," he whispered.

"Yes," she said, reaching for his belt, opening

it and finding his erection—hot, hard and ready for her.

"Make love to me, Henry," she said.

And he did. Taking her on his desk and making her completely his. He knew that no matter what else he thought about Malcolm Devonshire, without his father he wouldn't have found Astrid, and that was something he didn't know if he could have lived without.

Henry's lovemaking was fierce and all-consuming as always, but afterward when they'd cleaned up, he pulled her into his arms. She knew they had work to do. There was a lot going on every day, but now he just held her and stroked her back.

She rested her head against his shoulder and felt the kind of closeness she'd never had with another person before. Any person. She looked up at Henry and realized it was long overdue for her to tell him about Daniel and everything that had happened.

"What are you thinking?"

"That you stopped asking me about my secrets. Does that mean you no longer want to know them?"

"Not at all. I just decided that when you are ready to talk to me about them you will." He kissed her tenderly. "I think it's time to get back to work."

She nodded and stood up to leave. But she felt as though he'd pushed her away. She wondered if she'd gotten too close to him. She hoped not. She didn't want to end up like Kaye Allen, clinging to a man who no longer wanted her.

Astrid moved through the crowded Everest Mega Store. It was situated in Leicester Square, the heart of the touristy area of London. The store was packed today and Rona, the manager of this store, was beyond giddy at the fact. She looked like a retro punker with her nose ring and the four inch wide stripe of pink down the center of her hair.

"Your girl is nervous. She's in the storage area pacing around. She even left her guitar in the cab."

"Did you get it back?"

"Yes."

"I'll go talk to her," Astrid said.

Astrid took the elevator up to the third floor and entered the storage area. Steph was indeed pacing around but she seemed fine. No nerves to speak of.

"Hello, Astrid."

"How's it going, Steph? Ready for today?"

"I think so," Steph said. "This is how I always get before I go on. So don't worry that I'm going to wig out on you."

"I'm not worried at all. Do you know who Mo Rollins is?"

"I haven't been living under a rock," she said with a quick grin.

"He would say you are in great company based on your nerves. He always says the great ones worry they will never match the sound in their head and that's why they are nervous before they go out and perform."

Steph smiled. "Dang it, Astrid. I hadn't even worried about that. I'm just nervous because BBC Radio One is here and they want to interview me when I'm done singing."

"Didn't the media coach get you ready for that?"

"Yes, but practicing at home is different than actually doing it. And I don't want to sound like some kind of muppet."

"You won't. You're smart and poised. And Henry would never have produced an album for you if you weren't."

Steph hugged her. "Thank you. My boyfriend is supposed to be coming today but he got stuck at work."

"How'd you meet?" Astrid asked. The more

Steph talked the more she relaxed. And a relaxed artist would perform better.

"At university. We were both in elementary ed."

There was a rap on the door and one of the sound techs poked in his head. "We're ready for you in five minutes."

"Thanks." Steph went to fix her lipstick and the door opened. Astrid glanced over her shoulder to see Henry and Steven enter, talking quietly.

Henry winked at her, but didn't say anything as he went to talk to Steph. Astrid got a call on her cell from Rona that there was someone downstairs demanding to see Henry.

Astrid relayed the message. "I'll go see who it is and let you know if you are needed."

"Great. I'm switching my mobile to vibrate. Just send me a text, because I won't be able to hear a call. I don't like to be disturbed before a concert."

"Will do. Good luck, Steph," Astrid said as she walked to the door.

She stepped out onto the sales floor and saw that the Mega Store was impossibly busy today. Steven's business unit had to be making a fair profit. What would that mean for Henry?

She took the escalator down to the first floor where Rona waited. She pointed to the area near the registers. At first Astrid didn't recognize the woman, but as she got closer she realized it was Kaye—the woman from the rugby match.

"Hi. I'm Astrid Taylor, Mr. Devonshire's assistant. What can I do for you?"

Kaye gave her a scathing look. "Nothing. I need to talk to Henry."

Astrid tried to smile, but the other woman wasn't having any part of her friendliness.

"He won't have any free time today. If you give me your number, I'll have him call you tonight," Astrid said.

"He had my number," Kaye said.

"Fine. But if you give it to me then he won't have to search for it."

The other woman took a card from her handbag and handed it over. "It's urgent. I need to speak to him today."

"Very well. I will give him the message."

Kaye turned and walked away and Astrid watched the other woman go. She sent a text message to Henry informing him that Kaye was looking for him and giving him her number. She tried to shake off the negative feeling that meeting Kaye had produced in her. But it was hard.

She stood in the first floor crowd as Steph performed on the balcony area of the second floor. The acoustics in a retail shop weren't the best for a live performance, but the genuine quality of Steph's voice made up for that.

Astrid kept one ear on the music as she observed the people in the crowd. They really liked Steph's sound, and Astrid noted that as the performance wrapped up the queue to meet her grew. Her CD sales had been steadily high throughout the day.

Astrid went to the table where fans would be able to meet Steph and made sure everything was set up for her with bottles of water to drink, press photos to autograph. The digital photographer was there to take souvenir photos with any fan who wanted one.

Everything was perfect for the event and it cemented Astrid's belief that she and Henry were good at working together. But his reticence about the message from Kaye had her worried. Aside from the passion that was between them…what hold did she really have on him?

Henry left the mega store before Steph was finished performing. Kaye's message told him that this old girlfriend wasn't simply going to go away. And the underwear model had a bit of a temper, so if Henry didn't give her the attention she was demanding, he was afraid she'd do something to get his attention in another way.

Something that might involve Astrid. He didn't want that. He liked what he and Astrid had going. She brought a peace to his life he'd never found in another person.

Kaye answered her cell phone on the first ring. "It's about time you called me."

"What's up?" he asked her.

"I don't want to talk about this on the phone. Can you meet me?"

"Now?"

"Yes, now? This is urgent."

"Fine. Where are you?"

"There's a Café Europa around the corner from the Mega Store. Meet me there."

She hung up and Henry shoved his phone into his pocket.

"Everything okay?" Steven asked.

"No. I have to go take care of an urgent matter. Will you take care of Steph? Just get her down to Astrid and then she'll take over."

"I think I can handle that," Steven said in that wry way he had.

"I know you can. Thanks."

"No problem. Astrid is very efficient, isn't she? Do you think she'd like to work in retail?" Steven asked.

"No. She wouldn't like to work for anyone but me."

Steven laughed. "That's to the point."

"Indeed. But seriously she's interested in producing. I think she'll stay at the label for a long time."

"Good. I think she's a definite asset for the Everest Group."

Steven's comments demonstrated that the other man was thinking globally, thinking of the entire organization. And Henry realized that he didn't care quite so much about winning the chairmanship of the Everest Group. He liked running the record label. It suited him.

It was the first time in his life that he wasn't lusting after the next big thing. Was part of it to do with Astrid? Or had he simply found the place where he belonged?

That was an exhilarating thought. He walked out of the mega store and onto the street. There was the usual bevy of photographers, but none of them paid much attention to him as he walked away.

He found the coffee shop where Kaye waited at a table near the back.

"Hello, Henry."

He sat down next to her. "What is so urgent it couldn't wait?"

"I'm pregnant," she said.

Henry looked at her, trying to assess if she were lying. He was meticulous about birth control. Thanks to the circumstances of his own birth, he'd never wanted to have any kids without being committed to their mother.

"Are you sure?"

She gave him an exasperated look. "Of course I'm sure. Why wouldn't I be?"

"I have no idea. Look, sorry if I've offended you, I never expected to have this conversation. We were careful every time we were together," he said.

He sat back in his chair trying to see signs of her pregnancy in her body. She did seem a little fuller than she'd been before, but she wasn't thicker around the middle.

"How far along are you?" he asked.

"Four months."

Well, the timing was right for him to be the father. "What do you want from me?"

"I want you to support the child. I think it's the least you can do."

"Very well. Just have a paternity test and then

we can move forward. I'll have my lawyers get to work on drawing up some kind of paperwork for this," Henry said, running his hand through his hair. This he didn't need, but he'd never deny a child of his own. He wasn't going to make the same mistakes Malcolm had.

"I don't see why we need a paternity test," Kaye said.

"Because I'm a wealthy man, Kaye, and I'm not going to simply take your word. If the baby is mine we will move forward on my terms," Henry said. "But I would never deny a child of mine, and I will be a father to this baby if it is indeed mine."

"On your terms? I don't think so. I don't take orders from you."

"When it comes to the baby, you will," Henry said. "Together we'll make the decisions for the child."

"Fine," she said. "I'll arrange for the test to

be done as soon as I can. Will you stop dodging my phone calls?"

"Yes," he said.

Henry stood up to leave the café and walked back to the mega store with his mind in a mire of thoughts. *A child.*

He wasn't ready to be a father, he knew that. There was a reason why he'd been waiting to settle down. And there was only one woman he wanted to settle down with. Astrid.

How was she going to take the news that he might be a father?

"Henry?"

Astrid waited for him right inside the door of the retail store. There was a long queue still in front of Steph. This at least had been a huge success.

"Are you okay?"

"Yes. But we need to talk."

"Now?"

The retail store was jammed with industry

journalists and other insiders he should talk to. Did he put business on hold for a personal discussion?

No, he thought. This situation with Steph was easier to handle than talking to Astrid right now.

"No, it can wait until later," he said.

Astrid looked up at him with questions in her eyes, and he had that feeling in his gut that he wasn't meant to have the life he'd been wanting with this woman. If Kaye was pregnant with his child, he couldn't be with Astrid.

Unlike his father, he would do the right thing.

Eleven

Astrid sat tensely across from Henry as he talked to the waiter. Their table on a lovely balcony overlooking London and the dinner that they'd planned to celebrate Steph's success and that of the record label had taken on a different feel. She also planned to come clean about Daniel and her inability to have kids.

Henry hadn't been himself when he came back into the store earlier. His entire behavior had been cold and a bit distant since Steven had told her that Henry had to go take care of an urgent matter.

And having had an affair at work before, she was afraid of what the future held for her. Not just here with Henry—though if this relationship ended it would be very painful—but also with the musicians she'd come to know.

Finally the waiter left and Henry turned his attention to her. "I think you'll like the food here."

"I doubt it," she said.

"Why not?"

"Because I'm nervous. What did Kaye want?"

Henry leaned back in his chair. "I'm not sure how to say this except to just say it straight out."

"Go ahead then," Astrid said. She clenched her hands tightly on her lap. Even when Daniel had broke up with her, she had never dreaded the words that might come from a lover's lips. That said it all, didn't it?

"Kaye is pregnant and she believes I am the father."

Shock made her speechless. He couldn't have said he was going to be a father. "I'm sorry."

"I…I don't know what to do. Of course I can't just walk away the way Malcolm did. I want to be more to my kid than a check once a month and gifts at birthdays and Christmases."

His words were a death knell to her. Henry was exactly what she expected him to be. When she'd told Daniel was pregnant, he hadn't wanted any part of her life or her child's. When she'd lost that child, he'd fired her for attendance. And she'd walked away, feeling her faith in the goodness of men shaken. Somehow it wasn't surprising that Henry was the exact opposite.

"I can understand that. What are you thinking?" she asked.

"I've asked her to have a paternity test just to make sure the child is mine."

"Do you think there's a chance it might not be?"

Henry shrugged. "We were both dating other people as well as each other. So I'm not sure. I figure if Kaye came to me, she has to believe there's a good chance I'm the father."

"That makes sense. She wouldn't want to hit up her ex-boyfriends indiscriminately," Astrid said. Hoping she didn't sound bitter or angry, she knew she was. She'd found the man she wanted to spend the rest of her life with and had been trying to figure out how to move their relationship to the next level and now…now she had no idea what was going to happen.

"If the child is mine, we're going to have to marry, she and I."

He kept talking after that, but to be honest she didn't hear another thing he said. Why was he going to marry Kaye?

But she knew why. Henry had told her how he'd felt when Malcolm had largely ignored him, and she knew he wouldn't want his own child to grow up feeling that Henry hadn't wanted him.

But what about them?

"I can see that this is important to you…and I admire the fact that you are doing the right thing by your child."

"Do you?" he asked. "You seem like you don't care, Astrid."

"What do you want me to do?" she asked, very aware that she was holding on to her emotions, just barely. She wanted to cry or yell at him that marrying anyone for a child was a dumb mistake. But she couldn't do that because it was very clear Henry wanted to make up for his father's mistakes.

"I want—hell, I don't know. I want to know that it matters to you—that I matter to you."

"You matter more than you can imagine, Henry, but I know that you aren't a man who changes his mind. If you have decided to marry Kaye, then that's what you'll do."

He nodded. The waiter brought their food and Astrid had a surreal moment as she realized that life went on. Even though it felt as if her world had just ended, it was still going on around her.

"I can't do this," she said, standing up.

"Do what? There's no need for you to leave," Henry said.

"Yes, there is. I can't just sit here pretending that nothing has changed when everything has. Listen, Henry, this has been nice, but I should never have let this develop into more than a working relationship."

"You didn't let anything happen. We did it together. There is no reason to walk away. Kaye hasn't determined anything. We can continue as we have been," Henry said.

She shook her head. Continue? Until what?

"Think about what you just said. You plan to marry another woman *and* continue a relationship with me?"

Henry shook his head. "I sound like an idiot when I say that. But I don't want to give you up, Astrid."

"I can't do this," she said again. "I understand where you are coming from, but I can't live with a broken heart. I'm going to have to figure out what to do next."

Henry stood up, tossed some bills on the table and led her out of the restaurant. A part of her wanted him to make a big gesture, to say that he'd figure out a way to be involved in Kaye's child's life while still staying with her.

But she reminded herself as he pulled up to her building that she didn't believe in little-girl fantasies anymore. She was a real woman living a real life. And it seemed for her there was no happy ending.

Astrid left the restaurant and hailed a cab but when she got in, she dind't know where to tell him to go. Then she realized she needed her sister. Bethann was the absolute best at seeing through the crap and getting to the point. And as Henry's words kept repeating in her head and she felt the burn of tears at the back of her eyes she knew that she needed a shoulder t cry on.

"Where to, love?"

She gave the cabbie Bethann's address and sat back in the seat, unable to believe she had once again fallen for her boss. This time was so much worse. This time she knew she really loved Henry. An emotion that she'd tried to convince herself she felt for Daniel, but the words had always sounded hollow. Now she knew that with Henry it was the real deal.

How was she going to go on?

"Here you go, miss," the cabbie said.

She paid him and got out of the car. A light rain had started to fall as she stood on the street looking at her sister's townhouse. It was almost eleven, but she didn't hesitate as she walked up to the door and rang the bell.

The light came on over the door and a minute later she heard the key in the lock of the inner door.

"Who is it?" Percy asked.

"Astrid."

The door opened a minute later and Percy took one look at her face and sighed. "I'll get Bethann."

"Thank you," she said, following him into the sitting room.

He went up the stairs and less than a minute later Bethann came flying down the stairs. She wore a light blue nightgown with brown polka dots on it and her hair was in disarray, but the look on her face was fierce as she opened her arms and hugged Astrid.

"What happened? Do I need to get on the phone to his attorney and threaten him with some kind of lawsuit?" Bethann said.

Astrid shook her head. "No, Bethy, not that. He…"

She started crying as she tried to talk. She hated the way her voice deepened and the words just wouldn't come out. This was so not what she wanted from her life. She should have stayed firm in the vow she'd made to herself— no more men. That was what she'd said but somehow Henry Devonshire had managed to slip past her guard and into her heart.

"I don't know what to do."

"Tell me everything," Bethann said. She maneuvered them across the sitting room to the loveseat and drew Astrid down to sit next to her.

"His ex-girlfriend is pregnant and if the child is his, he is going to marry her."

"Oh, honey. I'm so sorry."

"I know. I understand why he's doing it—"

"I don't. I thought he was involved with you."

"He is," Astrid said. "But he won't give up a child of his. He doesn't want the child to grow up not knowing his father the way Henry did. I get that part of it. But the fact that he's going to marry her…."

"It is a noble thing to do," Bethann said. "Stupid but noble."

"He did say he'd like things to continue with me until he knew if he had to marry Kaye."

"Please tell me you said no."

"I'm not an idiot. Of course I did." Astrid felt tears welling in her eyes again. "The really dumb thing is I love him and I don't know how I'm going to stop."

Bethann hugged her close and rocked her in

her arms. "Stopping will be hard. You need something to concentrate on."

"Work. I am a career woman now," Astrid said.

"You were a career woman before," Bethann reminded her.

"But it's all I have now. I have to be focused on my job."

"Can you do it?"

Astrid thought about it long and hard. "I'm not sure but I have to try. I'm not about to lose another job because I fell in love with the wrong man."

Bethann agreed and then made up the sofa bed so that Astrid could spend the night there. After her sister went upstairs she heard the sound of her talking quietly to Percy and Astrid started to cry again, knowing that she wasn't going to have a man like that in her life. That she wasn't going to have Henry in her life anymore. And she knew she'd never be able to trust another man again. *Burn me once, shame on you*, she thought, *burn me twice, shame on me*. And she'd learned the hard way that love wasn't in the stars for her.

But work was. She was damned good at her career and if she played her cards right she'd be able to turn her job as Henry's assistant into one as a first-class producer. Nothing would keep her from achieving her goals...not now.

It took Henry about a day and a half to realize that letting Astrid walk out of his life was the biggest mistake he'd ever made. He couldn't imagine waking up next to Kaye every day. Even if he had his child there with them.

He knew that he was risking breaking the morality clause in Malcolm's damned agreement, but he didn't care. He simply couldn't marry Kaye to win a business deal. Business at the end of the day wasn't more important to him than family.

He dialed Kaye's number.

"It's Kaye."

"Hello, Kaye. I've been thinking a lot the past twenty-four hours about the baby and our possibly marrying."

"I've been thinking about it, too, Henry. I am so happy that you stepped up and did the right thing."

"I would never let a child of mine grow up without being a part of his or her life," Henry said. And those words were true. He had no doubts about being a father to Kaye's child.

That was one thing he'd realized about Malcolm and his mother's relationship—he didn't have to marry Kaye to still be the child's father. And unlike Malcolm he didn't see a personal life as an impediment to a successful life. In fact he thought that children would enhance his life and make it richer. His only doubts were of being a husband to the wrong woman.

"Great. I thought we could get married in Italy. I have a friend there who will lend us his villa. I think it will photograph nicely. I contacted a few friends at *Vogue*, and they have agreed to do a spread on us."

"No," Henry said. Finding the words to tell her he wouldn't marry her was harder than he expected.

"Well, fine. We can get married at your mum's place then. She has that fabulous country estate—"

"Kaye, stop. I'm not going to marry you."

"But you just said you wanted to be a father to my child."

"I do. I will. But I will not be doing it as your husband. We don't have to be married to raise a child."

"Henry, you *have* to marry me."

"No, Kaye, I don't."

"If you don't I'll make you regret it."

"Do your worst," he said and hung up the phone.

He wasn't too worried about Kaye. He'd

called his solicitor and asked the man to draw up a paternity agreement and a visitation schedule.

He spent the rest of the night trying to think of a way to win Astrid back. He knew he'd hurt her and he was determined to make it up to her. The next day he was surprised to receive a call from Edmond.

"We need to talk," Edmond said.

"Sure. Is this about the fact that my unit is outperforming the others?" Henry asked. He'd seen the financials. He was clearly the winner in the competition that Malcolm had set up for them.

"No, it's about Kaye Allen and you. Have you seen the papers this morning?"

"Not yet. Why?"

"There's a photo of Kaye with a prominent baby bump and the caption The Devonshire Legacy Lives On. Another Devonshire Is Refusing to Marry His Baby-Muma.

Henry cursed. His phone rand and he glanced at the caller ID. "Can you hold?"

"I'd rather not."

"My mum's on the other line."

"I'll wait," Edmond said.

Henry answered the call.

"Hi, Mum."

"Don't hi me, Henry Devonshire. I've spent the last thirty years doing my best to make sure that the world saw you as Henry Devonshire and not simply Malcolm's love child and then you do something like get a woman pregnant and refuse to marry her."

"Mum, we're not even sure the child is mine."

"What? Why not?"

"We had an open relationship."

"Does Astrid know?"

"Mum, I told her everything. I had intended

to marry Kaye but then realized I couldn't marry one woman when I wanted to share my life with another one."

There was silence on the line and then he heard her sigh. "Fine. But fix this and make it right."

"I will."

He hung up with his mum.

"Edmond?"

"I'm still here."

"Give me a few days to fix this. If I can't become CEO of the Everest Group, that's fine. But I'm not about to marry the wrong woman just to stave off gossip."

Again he hung up. He went downstairs and got the papers, reading them. Unfortunately Kaye's announcement had reawakened the frenzy that had started with the birth of him and his brothers.

* * *

Astrid wouldn't take his calls, and no matter what he did in his personal life he couldn't get it on track.

The results of the paternity test came back a week later, revealing that he wasn't the father of Kaye's child. Henry was relieved, but he'd screwed up his relationship with Astrid. No matter what he said to her, he couldn't fix that.

Since she wouldn't talk to him privately, he had an idea to do a public interview. He called a friend at BBC and arranged to do an interview about his biological father along with Steven and Geoff. The other men readily agreed because they were tired of seeing those old pictures of their mums showing up in the newspapers.

Henry hoped seeing the interview would make Astrid take his calls.

They all wanted a chance to put a new face

on the scandal that the men's births had caused. The interview went well and his own mum met a producer who had heard about her game show and wanted to work with her. Tiffany Malone was over the moon. He was her golden boy once again, and he was happy to be back on good terms with his mum but he really longed to be back with Astrid.

He'd known from the beginning that he wanted her in his life. And that she was different from all the other women he'd dated, but he hadn't realized how much until they'd been apart. He missed so much of her.

Her keen smile, her sassy wit and her sexy body had won him over. He couldn't sleep at night because his arms felt empty without her.

Winning her back wasn't easy. After she continued not taking his calls, he'd tried to contact her family, but her parents were out of town. Bethann took one call from him only to curse him out.

He rubbed the back of his neck. A lesser man would give up, but Henry wasn't a quitter and he didn't intend to back down now.

The first copy of the XSU studio sessions were delivered to his office and he remembered the first night they'd heard the group play. That night had changed everything between them.

Astrid saved every message that Henry left on her answering machine. It would have been so nice if she could have instantly fallen out of love with him, Then she'd be able to really move on. Instead, each time she heard his voice she cried a little from missing him.

But she couldn't continue to be his mistress while he married another woman. Yet once she read in the newspapers that he wasn't going to marry Kaye and then when she'd learned his was going to appear on BBC One in an interview with Steven and Geoff...well, she couldn't resist the chance to see him.

Henry looked tired, she thought, as she watched the program. But he carried himself well in the interview as the reporter asked each of them questions about the scandal that had surrounded their births.

"Our mums all loved Malcolm Devonshire," Henry said. "He just loved the Everest Group more."

"Now each of us is running part of that company," Geoff added, "And we understand the difficulties of being in charge of a huge conglomerate and keeping up a personal life."

"And we can see why the media is so interested in us and our mothers. We've never really been together before this, but we hope that your curiosity about us is appeased," Steven said.

"Because we all have lives we'd like to get back to living outside of the spotlight," Henry concluded.

The rest of the interview focused on the three men, their mothers and how the boys had been raised. It was interesting to her and she saved it on her DVR so she could watch it again, which she did several times over the next few days.

Henry called again and told her voice mail that he wasn't the father of Kaye's baby and he needed to talk to her. And she wanted to talk to him, but now the fact that she'd never told him she couldn't have a child was at the forefront of her mind.

Having a child of his own was important to Henry and that was the one thing she couldn't give him.

Henry knew what to do.

It took him a few days to wrangle everyone into place, but on Friday night he drove to Woking with a framed photo of the two of them and an engagement ring in his pocket. He got there as everyone was getting home from work.

He had called the building manager and

confirmed that Astrid was indeed at home, even though she refused to take his calls.

He also called Bethann, who was waiting for him when he arrived. He was surprised to see she wasn't carrying a pitchfork or accompanied by an angry mob.

"This better work," she said.

"No one wants that more than I do."

Success didn't matter without Astrid by his side. He needed her. They needed each other—together they were whole. And he wasn't going to back down.

XSU arrived twenty minutes later and Henry had the band set up. He just needed the confirmation that she was inside the flat itself. Bethann called up and Astrid did answer.

Now that he knew where she was, nothing could stop him from winning her back.

He remembered every big game he'd played and every big event in his life and how much he'd wanted to win. They all paled in comparison to what he wanted now. What he needed now.

Astrid.

"I'm going to go up and open her window so she can hear the band. Give me about ten minutes to talk to her."

Henry nodded. "Thank you, Bethann."

"You're welcome. Just make my sister happy for the rest of her life and we'll call it even."

"I intend to."

Bethann walked away, and a small crowd gathered as the band tuned up their instruments. Henry ignored them as his mum and stepdad arrived with his younger brothers.

"I'm glad you got here."

"Wouldn't miss it. I like Astrid. If you are going to ask her to marry you, we want to be a part of it."

He hugged his mum close realizing how lucky he had been to have been born her son. Percy brought Astrid's parents. It had taken him a while to track them down and to tell them what had happened. He wanted Astrid to become his with the blessing of her family and his.

Finally he saw the window to Astrid's flat open, and he signaled the band, who started playing. He waited where he was until he saw Astrid's pretty blond head peek out the window. She looked down at him and covered her mouth with one hand.

Bethann appeared beside her, wrapping her arm around her sister's shoulder. When the band finished playing, Henry took the microphone from Angus but before he could speak Astrid did.

"Go home, Henry. This isn't going to do anything except make us both look ridiculous."

"That's not true. I'm here to set things right."

"How? There's no way you can do that."

"Not even if I tell you that I love you?"

* * *

Astrid wasn't sure she'd heard Henry properly. She knew he'd been trying to apologize since the day he'd told her he was going to marry another woman, but she'd steeled herself against those words. She knew that Henry was the one man on the earth that she loved with her entire heart and soul.

The pain he'd caused her had been deep, and she wasn't ready to forgive him. At first a part of her wanted him to suffer, but that hadn't made her feel any better. And then she'd been afraid to take his calls.

She'd watched the special on BBC just like everyone else. A part of her had felt a twinge of hope when he'd told the interviewer that he was involved with a special woman.

Now he was standing in the car park at her flat with the very band that had played the night they'd kissed. And he was looking up at her as if she mattered to him.

But she was afraid to believe in him. Afraid to get hurt again.

"You love me? What if—"

"Don't say anything else," Henry said. "Let me come up."

She noticed her parents and brother-in-law, Percy, were standing down there next to Henry. And Tiffany and Gordon and Joshua and Lucas were there, as well. He'd brought their families together.

"Okay," she said.

She looked around her familiar apartment with its open floor plan and IKEA furniture. She'd done her best to make this place into her home. There were pictures of her family on the wall and she felt safe here. It was the place she retreated to when she needed to escape from the world as she had when she'd miscarried.

This was where she'd been reborn. And she wasn't too sure she could do it again. There were only so many times she could recover from having her heart broken and she didn't want to have to do it again. Not with Henry.

She stepped back from the window. "I think he really loves me."

Bethann started laughing. "I think so, too, but only you can decide that. I'm going to go down and wait with Percy and Mum and Dad."

"Bethy?"

"Yes?"

"How did you know for sure about Percy?"

"He's the only man to make me feel alive. He's not perfect, but he's mine and when I look at him I know that he loves me even when I'm being a cow."

She hugged her sister as she left and thought about what Bethann had said. Love was more than just that grand illusion. It was about the quiet times when no one else watched.

Henry knocked on her door and she opened it for him. He handed her a wrapped present as he came inside. Through the open window she still heard the sound of XSU playing.

"You didn't have to bring a gift for me," she said.

"Yes, I did. I missed you every day," he said. He reached for her and drew her into his arms.

"This last week has been the longest of my life," Henry said. "I can't believe I was so stupid to think I could marry another woman when you own my heart."

She looked up at him and saw the truth in his eyes. Saw that he believed what he was saying. "I...I'm afraid to believe that you are really going to stay. So many times I've been left before."

"I know that. But I'm not like the other men you've loved before."

She shook her head. "I haven't loved any man before. Not like I love you."

"I love you, too, Astrid and I want to make

a life with you. I want to get married and have children. I want us to continue to build our life together."

She wanted that, too, but Henry would have to know the truth. "I can't have children, Henry. I…I had an ectopic pregnancy and it was complicated. I lost the baby and my doctor warned that I…well, I can't have any kids."

Henry hugged her close. "As long as I have you I'm happy. You're the missing piece to this life I've made for myself. It didn't take me any time at all to realize that without you by my side nothing mattered."

He reached into his pocket and brought out a jewelers' box and got down on one knee in front of her. "Astrid Taylor, will you marry me?"

She looked down at him. At the man she'd had a crush on when she was teenage girl and the boss she'd thought was such a cutie and realized that the man he was, was so much more than that.

"Yes, Henry Devonshire, I will marry you."

He put the ring on her finger as he stood up and kissed her.

He went to the window and looked down at their family.

"She said yes."

They applauded and Astrid laughed, happy to have finally found the man she'd always searched for.

* * * * *